Wind Never Forgets

Letters From A Father To His Daughter

Veera Raghavan

Also by Veera Raghavan

Love Arrived

Love Arrived – The Journey

Naked Indian in White Sneakers

Lipstick on My Coffee Mug

To Isha—my daughter, my light, my anchor, my wild heart, my greatest lesson in love. Your presence redefines my understanding of love every single day.

You are the reason for these words, the force behind every reflection, and the soul of this book.

And to my son in absence, whose presence in memory continues to shape me in ways I am still uncovering.

This book is a piece of our story—of love, loss, and survival. It is my way of telling you: I was here, I lived, I loved, and I left something behind for you.

To my family—those who shaped me, broke me, rebuilt me, and loved me through it all. This book carries pieces of you in every chapter.

To Charles Bukowski and Pablo Neruda, whose raw, unfiltered words and fiery verses lit the spark that fuels my love for writing.

To those who held space for me in my darkest moments, who offered quiet support, loud laughter, or simply stayed. You know who you are.

To the reader—thank you for holding these words, for allowing them to exist beyond me.

Contents

For you, **Isha**.

Isha, I owe you this truth—I once thought of leaving. I had let the weight of my pain convince me that there was no way forward, that the only escape was to disappear. But I was wrong. It was a cowardly thought, and I regret ever allowing it space.

I wanted to take the easy way out because I didn't have the courage to face my situation. And for that, I am sorry. Sorry for even considering abandoning you in a world where you should never have to feel alone.

But I am still here. I am grateful I did not act on those thoughts, and I vow to myself—to you—that I never will again.

Isha, my dear,

I started writing letters to you from a time of darkness in my life—a period so bleak that I thought I wouldn't make it through those days.

At first, I couldn't even form full sentences—just fragmented thoughts and apologies, words that felt empty. I had things to say, but I couldn't yet find my voice. The pages were smudged with tears, and I couldn't bring myself to write what truly mattered.

I wanted to tell you what kind of father I was, what kind of father I could have been—but the grief was too much, and the letters remained unfinished.

I was also reflecting on the life I had lived, not just on the darkness and pain. They were my attempt to make sense of life, a way to grasp clarity by reaching for the stories of our family.

I started writing by hand. Writing by hand has a quality to it—it feels different: slower, deliberate, unfiltered. It forces surrender to the moment as your hand struggles to keep pace with thoughts and memories. I found myself reaching places I didn't expect—digging up grief I thought I had buried. I uncovered happiness I hadn't let myself feel. And I found strength I didn't know I still carried.

Over time, I realized these weren't just fragments of my thoughts or struggles; they were pieces of something bigger—our family, our history, and everything that made us who we are. These letters are not instructions, nor are they a roadmap for your life. They are reflections—moments of learning and unlearning. And what began as a private reflection slowly became something meant for you.

There was a time when the world had lost its color for me, like I was losing my place in it. But even in those moments, one thing kept me here—you. Thinking of you, of the person you might grow to be, reminded me that I still had something to say, something to leave behind.

These letters are my attempt to capture who we are—who you are, who I am, who your mother and grandparents were. They're stories of love and struggle, of battles fought and joys celebrated.

This isn't a story of miracles or redemption. There was no moment when the sun came out, and the darkness vanished. Coming back was slow and painful—a crawl, one uncertain step at a time. But in those steps, I learned truths about life, pain, and the strength that persists even when everything feels broken.

As you read these, remember this: you come from a long line of survivors, dreamers, and fighters. You carry their strength, their flaws, and their hopes in your blood. These stories are yours to carry.

I'm starting with the darkness I'm in. It's not easy to write about, but it matters. Because even in our darkest moments, the essence of who we are remains—we're still us. And I want you to know me completely—not just the parts that are easy to share.

I wasn't sure if I'd make it through, but I did. I want you to have these pieces of our story, of our history. They're not always pretty. Sometimes, they're messy, painful even. But they're real, and they're ours.

Some of these letters come from long after the night I decided to keep going. Others were written in the depths of darkness and later revisited, shaped by hindsight. But I've left some rawness in many to reflect on the nights I had to navigate through to become the father and the person you see today.

So here it is—the beginning of our story, with the hardest chapter of my life. I hope that by sharing my struggle, you'll find something that speaks to your own journey.

Your Appā

⟨∿⟩ ⟨∿⟩ ⟨∿⟩

Isha,
Didn't think it would come to this,
I was a fool to let a stranger show me the river,
I was naive to give my dream my last dime to a lie,
And crying doesn't make it go away anymore,
I have done the crime,
And I don't know what more I can do to see the light again,

Leaving you seems so wrong now,
It's too late.
It's too late to make that call,
It's already inside me, running through my veins,
It's burning out the fire still left in me,
I can feel it in my eyes,
I can taste and smell it now,
Goodbye.

There is a darkness in my soul, and it has spread into my veins,
But what more can I do,
I am too far gone to see how it ends,
Too tired to fight this anymore,
I don't want to lose to the demons calling my name again and
again,
I am tired.
I am tired.

But then again, you are the only pulse holding me tonight,
But for you, I'll hold on through this,

How cruel would I be
to let your tears call out my name,
And leave you in someone else's hands,
I'll fight this darkness to be your light.

〰 〰 〰

The Night You Saved Me

It was the night I had planned to die. 2 AM. Sydney.

I'm still awake, sitting on the balcony of your grandparents' house, staring into the horizon, into the nothingness, and at the Sydney skyline. The city looks like a postcard—calm, distant, untouchable. At night, the city shines like a bride's mother—well past her prime, yet still lingering in the limelight. Whatever is said of the city, Sydney has always been my home. I'm grateful for everything for all it has given me, and now, I'm relieved to be back here with our family.

This has become my nightly ritual over the past few months. It feels strange to call this a ritual, but that's what it's become. Every night, I sit here with my thoughts, waiting for the hours to pass, waiting for something to change. Sleep had become a stranger to me for a while now, and at this point, I've stopped chasing it.

We've been staying here since we returned from Singapore, waiting for the tenants to vacate our own place. Their home is beautiful, close to the bay, with a view of the city—a view that represents years of their hard work. And they have filled it with love. But it doesn't feel like home. I carry too much guilt to feel at home anywhere.

I know I've let you and your mother down. I made a mistake by trusting my finances to friends, and their betrayal is something I've struggled to bear. I've been paying for it ever since. I've replayed it all in my head—the warnings I ignored, the signs I didn't see. But no amount of regret can undo the fact that I failed. The betrayal hurts, but it's the guilt that's killing me. I thought I could protect us. I thought I'd never let you or your mother suffer because of me. But here we are.

These past months, my thoughts have been consumed by vengeance, failure, and guilt. I've let myself go, both physically and emotionally. I'm glad that we're all back home, but I can't seem to find peace. Sleep, when it comes, is often cut short by nightmares. A deep-rooted fear has taken hold of me, growing so strong that I've stopped smiling.

Honestly, I don't miss sleep much anymore. Staying up offers a strange kind of comfort, especially at night. The night provides a refuge—a time when the pressures of the day fade away. The night asks nothing of you but acceptance. In its stillness, darkness, and silence, one can sense it cradling a seed, waiting for the first light, a hope, or a thought to come and nourish it. I've always been a night owl; the darkness never scared me. The silence of the night has always given me the stillness and space I need to explore my thoughts and write. The night itself is a storyteller, patiently waiting to unravel its secrets.

Tonight feels different. I can't keep pretending things will get better. I've spent months trying to find a way out of this, and the only option that makes sense is to leave. I told myself it would be better this way—that if I disappeared, you and your mother would finally be free of the weight I bring into every room.

It had rained heavily that evening, leaving the air crisp and clean. Now, the clouds had mostly cleared, making the night feel magical in a way I hadn't expected. A soft, warm glow filled the sky and air—not quite twilight, but something gentler. It didn't take away the darkness; it lingered within it, casting just enough light to make the night feel alive, almost sacred. There was a strange sense of comfort that the night didn't disappoint—it felt fitting for what would be my last night alive. I don't know what it was, but in that moment, I felt some kind of peace.

Beside me, I had a laptop with handwritten letters to you, notes to your mother, and a few drawings carefully tucked inside.

I sat out here for hours, trying to make peace with the decision. I'd been drinking gin all night—and it helped. It softened the edges of my fear and made the whole thing feel distant and logical. The bottle was nearly empty, the tonic flat, but I kept drinking anyway. I've never been one to waste a good drink.

Gin wasn't my usual choice, but I had recently developed a taste for it. As I savored the drink, a speck of light caught my eye, moving quickly across the sky. I presumed it to be the Hubble Telescope. It wasn't anything important, just a faint glow against the darkness. But I couldn't stop watching it. Maybe it was comforting to see something so small still moving. Still doing what it was meant to do. It was more than I felt capable of.

The vastness of space has always intrigued me, and I felt a small sense of satisfaction that, on my last night, my lifelong fascination with the cosmos seemed to settle in this small, moving point of light, as if everything I had ever wondered about found its place.

It was getting chilly, and I glanced into the bedroom where you and your mother were asleep. The lamp on my side of the bed was still on—I've always needed some light to sleep. I felt an urge to walk in and touch your heads, but I hesitated, not wanting the cold drift to wake you. I had kissed both of you before you went to sleep and had whispered a soft goodbye to you, my sweet daughter. Now, it was time to make peace with myself and with the fact that I wouldn't be here in the morning.

Treachery had broken me, shattering everything I once believed in and leaving me trapped in deep distrust. Finding a way forward felt impossible, and the thought of ending it all seemed like the only escape. I knew it was a cowardly thought, but I had already gone through countless cycles of introspection and self-judgment. My heart felt torn apart while my soul and mind wandered into unfamiliar, dark places. I had never experienced such darkness before, and just when I thought it couldn't get any worse, the weight of despair only grew heavier.

In those moments of darkness, I began to write letters to you, my 18-month-old daughter. Letters that sometimes contained nothing but your name and a simple "sorry" beside it. Most were drenched in tears as I tried to express the kind of man I was and the father I wished I could have been.

I began to cry. I had thought that by now, all my tears would have dried up, making it easier to pass away in the darkness. But it wasn't easy. The guilt consumed me more than the fear, and the sense of abandoning my responsibilities weighed heavily on me.

The early morning birds had started to chirp, signaling that the night was coming to an end. I gathered the laptop and the letters, carefully placed them in a plastic pouch, and quietly walked back into the bedroom. I slipped in quietly, my footsteps careful and measured, trying not to disturb the stillness of the room, and placed the pouch on my bedside table. You had shifted in your sleep; you were now lying horizontally, taking up more space than anyone your size should, with your legs draped over your mother as you always do, facing me. You looked angelic. I stood there for a long time, watching the two of you.

I sat on the bed, gently pushed you over, and lay down next to you. I touched your hair, and the tears began to flow again. I kissed you and wanted to whisper goodbye, but all I could muster was a quiet "I'm sorry," repeated over and over. The tears dripped onto you, but I couldn't stop them. "You were my baby, my sweetheart." Your breathing was soft and regular, each exhale a reminder of how simple and beautiful life should be.

I sobbed quietly, and in those moments, nothing mattered but being next to you. I kissed you a few times, spooned you, and adjusted to get as close as possible. I was ready to leave, at peace with my decision to die. But I still hadn't come to terms with leaving you and your mother behind alone.

I turned off the light. The early sun was beginning to break through the darkness. I sat up, watching the sky light up. At some point, you had shifted in your sleep and were now holding my finger—your small hand wrapped around my left ring finger as you slept blissfully.

The weight of your hand—the weight of what it meant, the trust you had in me, even in your sleep, hit me. That trust, that innocence, made me realize how much I had left to fight for. It wasn't about fixing the past anymore; it was about showing up for the future.

What was I leaving behind? A string of failures? A family I'd broken? Or was I abandoning something far more important— hope, trust, love? The questions tore at me, but I told myself it was too late.

At that moment, everything I had told myself crumbled. The story I'd repeated in my head—that I was a failure, that there was nothing left for me—sounded hollow when you gripped my hand. You didn't know my pain or my guilt. All you knew was that I was your Appā, the one you reached for even in your sleep. "You didn't ask if I was worthy; you just asked that I stay." That simple trust was more powerful than any fear I carried. It was all you needed, and somehow, it became enough for me, too.

I thought of the first time you gripped my finger in the hospital, your tiny hand wrapped around it as if it were your anchor to the world. That same hand now held mine, unknowingly pulling me back from the edge. You had always trusted me without question.

How could I break the trust you had in me? Thoughts flooded my mind, questioning the fairness of what I was about to do. I realized that in trying to punish myself for the treachery I had experienced, I was about to commit an act of treachery against my own family. I didn't want you to go through the same darkness. I didn't want you to be at the mercy of anyone else. What kind of life was I pushing you into?

This wasn't the first time I'd stood at this edge. There had been nights before, quieter but no less heavy when the thought of ending it all whispered at the edges of my mind. But somehow, I'd always stepped back, telling myself there might be something waiting for me on the other side of tomorrow. This night, though, felt different. I'd run out of excuses, run out of strength to believe that I could make things right.

It wasn't just the thought of leaving—I told myself it was time to stop dragging others into my mess, to step away with whatever dignity I had left. But even as I thought it, the word stung. How could there be dignity in running away? There's no dignity in disappearing, no heroism in leaving others to clean up the mess. I wasn't choosing dignity—I was choosing escape. And as I sat there, that realization stung more than the thought of staying.

I thought about what my absence would mean—not just to you, Isha, but to everyone who still held a piece of me in their hearts. Was I about to pass on the same pain I had carried? The thought of leaving something so heavy behind made me pause. Was I ready to let that be my legacy?

A need to be there for you made me think that maybe, just maybe, I should give life another chance—or give myself another chance—

for you. As I sat there, I realized the decision wasn't about fixing everything I had broken. It was about showing up, even in my imperfections, for the people who needed me most. And then, in your sleep, you reached for my hand and pulled it close to your chest.

It wasn't a grand epiphany or a flash of light—it was just your tiny hand, a small reminder of what love looks like when it's pure and unearned. You didn't even know you'd saved me, but you did. And for that, I'll always be grateful.

I kissed you on the head and made the decision to live for you. I gently patted your mother's head; she didn't stir. She had seen me suffer and was probably bracing herself for the uncertainties ahead, with or without me in your lives. I planted a kiss on her forehead and stood up.

I took the pouch from the table and carefully placed it under the bed. Then, I headed downstairs. Milo, our dog, was sleeping soundly and didn't bother waking up. I couldn't blame him; it was still very early. I put on my running shoes and stepped outside. The night was now well and truly over. The darkness had dispersed.

I was going to be here to face it, to be the light instead of the darkness I was about to push my family into.

That night didn't fix me, but it reminded me of something I'd forgotten: even when we feel lost, love can anchor us. And sometimes, that's enough to keep going. It didn't take away the weight I carried or the mistakes I'd made. But it gave me something to hold on to. Something I didn't know I was still capable of having: hope.

We all have moments when the darkness feels too big to handle when it feels like letting go would be easier than staying. But sometimes, all it takes is one small act—a hand holding yours, a moment of stillness—to remind us why we stay. For you, I stayed.

You didn't know it, but you saved me that night. And for that, I'll always be grateful.

Yours always, Appā

Part 1: Beginnings
(roots, identity, transformation)

Isha, everything begins somewhere. These letters, my story, even the person you are becoming—it all starts from something small and grows. My roots shaped me long before I understood them, and the choices I made—both willingly and unwillingly—were influenced by the place I came from. Some of these memories are crystal clear, others are fragments, but together, they make up the truth of where I come from and how I became the man I am today.

As you read this, you may find pieces of yourself in my journey. Maybe you'll recognize the pull of identity, the tension between where you come from and where you're headed. Maybe you'll see the echoes of your own transformation taking shape. Take what you need, and let the rest settle where it may.

Every family has a story to tell,
And within your family, a rich collection of stories resides,
A vast network of connections on both sides,
Countless narratives waiting to be unveiled.
Some stories remain hidden, veiled in secrecy,
While others are shared, recounted time and again,
Some hold profound meaning, whispered every fortnight,
And some are simply whimsical, pure, and plain.
These stories don't have recounts of mountain scalers or seas conquerors,
Nor do of elephant hunters or pirate escapades,
Instead, they speak of generations who endured invasions, treachery, hardships, and dark days.
These stories celebrate small victories and moments of joy,
They carry the essence of hope for you in the future,
Embrace them.
Respect that.
You are now part of that story.
A story that you will take further when I depart.
Have pride in that.
Our families for generations have
depended on the sun, the rain,
the land,
and the stars lining up.
they stayed close to home,
married through allegiance and
at death turned to ash.
Some spirited souls, though, preferred to be buried,
but none get a marked grave.
All are fine with it.

No shrine to grieve when there is a life and a belonging to
celebrate.
Simple life.
My family are shepherds, tied to the land and the rivers flowing
into the southern side of the Bengal Bay,
Your mother's family are farmers, tied to the land and the sea in
the Western Ghats.
I have never herded.
Nor has your mother ever farmed.
But the spirit to celebrate belonging remains,
and will continue through you.
Cherish life. Keep it simple. Celebrate family.
Stay true to who you are, Isha.

⟪∿⟫ ⟪∿⟫ ⟪∿⟫

Our Tribe Lives On Through You

Dear Isha,

When I was 24, I took my first real trip. It's not that I hadn't traveled before; I had, but it was always with my family to our ancestral village, Mangadu. Every summer, our family packed almost everything from our house in Bangalore and visited my Nan's house in Mangadu. While my friends visited beaches, fairs, national parks, and zoos, our destination remained the same. Despite this, Mangadu filled me with a sense of belonging, even if it didn't spark wonder.

Mangadu is a small, enchanting place nestled on the banks of the Palar River, not far from the historic city of Kanchipuram. At first glance, Mangadu might seem like any other village in Tamil Nadu, but its timelessness reflects the enduring spirit of a community deeply connected to its land and heritage. The village, with its 40 thatched houses lining dirt streets and a small marketplace with 7 shops and 2 tea stalls, is lush with green fields, swaying coconut palms, and vibrant paddy patches. The air is heavy with the scent of jasmine, the smell of cow dung, and the earthy aroma of fertile red soil—a stark contrast to the city I was used to.

As the summer sun climbed, the heat and humidity would cover us in a constant sweat, wearing people down. Life moved slowly; most afternoons were spent idling under the shade of neem and banyan trees or gathering in courtyards. By March, the Palar River would run dry, offering no relief from the heat until sunset. This relentless heat was a constant point of contention between my parents and me, but their promises to take me elsewhere the following summer kept me going.

In the evenings, Mangadu transformed. The village came alive with the glow of oil lamps and the fragrance of burning incense. The marketplace turned into a riot of colors and aromas, as vendors enticed passersby with the scent of freshly made vadai and parottas, and the glimmer of bangles and hair ribbons. But it was at my Nan's house where the real magic happened. We kids played kabaddi in the courtyard, and the aroma of simmering sambar, deep-frying appālams, and ripe mangoes filled the air. Seated on the floor, we waited for the food to be served on banyan or siali leaf plates, and after the meal, someone would share stories of our ancestors or mythical tales. On full moon nights, fables were enacted with masks (koothu) and the sound of drums and conchs. The heat, the stench, the dirt, and the dullness of life would dissolve, replaced by a sense of enchantment.

Mangadu was more than just a place—it was the root of who I was. But roots don't hold us back; they push us forward. Like my father before me, I felt the pull to leave, to find something beyond the familiar. From this small village, my father and his father before him set out to explore and work, eventually making their way to Madras. This urge to explore lived in me as well. Family circumstances meant I didn't travel much by myself until my twenties, but I knew I was meant to see the world. The idea of stepping into the unknown thrilled me.

When the opportunity to migrate to Australia presented itself, I seized it. Mom wasn't excited; she worried about me heading off on my own, knowing I wouldn't be coming back. While it's common in our community for adult children to remain close to home, both Mom and I sensed that my path would lead me further afield.

As the day to leave approached, I felt a tug at my heart, a real anxiety about leaving everything familiar behind. I didn't speak to anyone about it, and it showed when I overpacked, unsure of what to expect. At the airport, I looked at my bags and realized I was carrying too much—more than just luggage. It was supposed to be a fresh start, yet I felt the weight of everything I was leaving behind.

2.

I took a late-night flight from Bangalore to Melbourne, transiting through Singapore for a few hours. In Singapore, I felt the full weight of my decision. For the first time, I was completely on my own, with no familiar faces in sight. I hadn't told my sister, who worked for Singapore Airlines, that I was transiting through Singapore. On a whim, I called her from a public phone, my heart pounding. When she answered, it felt like I'd found a piece of home in the middle of everything unfamiliar. I was thrilled to hear she was nearby and could come to the airport.

When she arrived, I broke down. Tears came before words. She didn't understand why, but I did. I was stepping into a new life, leaving everything I knew behind. Holding her in that embrace, I let everything out and left three carry-on bags with her.

As I handed my sister those carry-ons, my hands trembled. It wasn't just the weight of the bags I was shedding—it was the safety of everything I'd ever known. I felt stripped bare. The weight of my old life was gone, but what replaced it wasn't freedom—it was vulnerability.

It was the end of who I had been and the beginning of who I was going to be. Those tears mixed joy with the stark realization of the new path ahead—an opportunity I grasped with both hands. It meant leaving my parents, my hometown, and all my childhood memories for a chance at a better life.

It was also the day I stopped using my middle name as my first name—the name that had shaped my identity until then. A new me, a fresh name, and a new country.

Moving to a new country isn't just about new streets and maps—it's about losing parts of yourself and discovering what replaces them. The streets of Melbourne felt off at first, the sidewalks too clean, the shopkeepers too polite, no sounds of honking, no rush of humanity around me, and even the sky looked too open.

I didn't know how to navigate conversations. They were awkward. I was very conscious of my accent. The nights felt lonely. But slowly, things changed, and in the process I discovered strength I didn't know I had.

Isha, home isn't a place you find—it's something you create. Sydney became home when I stopped trying to replicate what I had left behind and started embracing what was in front of me. It happened in moments—sharing meals with new friends, navigating quiet streets that once felt daunting, and watching the light reflect off the harbor. In these moments, a new life took shape.

Life is mysterious, Isha. It presents situations that reveal new worlds and dimensions we never knew existed. When you're prepared and intent on moving forward, life offers opportunities to step into something new. That step was my chance to start over in a new land, leading to experiences that have shaped my personality and understanding of the world.

The urge to move, to explore, is in our blood. From Mangadu to Madras, my father, and his father before him sought better lives beyond the horizon. I felt that same pull, as did the ancestors who came before us. This drive to push forward, to leave the familiar in search of something greater, is a part of who we are.

3.

Isha, in our ancestral village, Mangadu, there's a big rock, the 'Yānaikal,' right by a temple. Its name comes from its elephant-shaped head. This rock stands as a silent witness to the dreams and aspirations of our forefathers. I often imagine them sitting on that rock, gazing at the horizon, contemplating their future and the futures of their children. The rock knows it all—plans, dreams whispered, betrayals buried, hopes left behind, and everything in between.

I visited that rock after my father passed away. His death left me with a profound sense of loss, and I needed to process my grief in my own way. One evening, I sat on the rock, watching the sunset, tracing my father's footsteps, acknowledging their role in shaping my life, and honoring the legacy I continue.

Next to Yānaikal stands a small but ancient temple dedicated to Lord Shiva, built of white stones. The murals of deities on the temple walls, though worn away by moisture, can still be seen. The lingam sits in the center, surrounded by idols that have been smoothened by time. Shepherds and passers-by enter the temple these days only to take refuge from the hot sun.

But our ancestors weren't worshipers of Sivan. It's not that they don't have faith in this god, but their devotion is directed toward Vishnu, one of the other gods in the holy Hindu trinity. And with no other Vishnu temples nearby, suggesting our ancestors were migrants to this part of the world and to Mangadu. Standing in the temple, I wondered: what brought our ancestors here? To this place, to this god? Their migrations mirrored my own, driven by a need to adapt and find new belonging. Their courage to embrace the unknown gave me the strength to find belonging, not by recreating what was left behind but by building something new.

Just as our ancestors found belonging in Mangadu through their faith, I realized that my sense of home in Sydney would come not from replicating what I left behind but from embracing what was ahead.

I pondered over my own origins—Who do I think I am? Was I Tamil, or did my roots come from the North or perhaps from Africa, as they say all humans originated? Could we be descendants of the lost continent of Kumari Kandam?

This journey of self-discovery isn't just about age; it's about tracing our paths and understanding the migration and travels defining our family. Our history is marked by a relentless pursuit of a place to call home, a narrative that has been part of our family for generations.

I scoured research papers and forums to trace our family name's origins. I found common threads among families sharing our dialect, rice preferences, ornaments, forehead markings, dietary restrictions, type of sarees and veshtis we wear, and how we wear them. This led me to trace our migration path north of the Eastern Ghats to a king in mythology: Prince Yadu. Cast out by his father for refusing to exchange his years of youth, forged his own path, and those who followed him were the Yadavas.

Somewhere along this lineage, my father's ancestors came from the Ponni River belt in the south, making their way inland. My mother's side, however, likely traveled down from the Narmada Valley, carrying with them traditions shaped by the landscapes they left behind. Two migrations—one moving north to south, the other south to further south—eventually converged. And though time blurred the origins, fragments of their journey still exist in the customs we hold, the language we speak, and the way we belong to the land.

You're a Yadava, too, Isha. From Mangadu's quiet streams to Bangalore's bustling streets and now to Sydney, I've traveled far. Moving is part of who we are, woven into our blood. I've made many places my home, and I take pride in that.

Isha, this legacy of journeying and discovery is yours to carry forward. You come from a long line of travelers, each venturing beyond the known world of our time—your mother and I included. We've built lives in new places, forming the foundation of your own. This urge to move, explore, and adapt is a flame passed down to you. I hope it burns brightly within you.

Home isn't just where we are born—it's the places that shape us, the stories we carry, and the people who hold us close. From the green fields of Mangadu to the city streets of Bangalore, I have traveled far. And now, here you are, in Sydney, carrying forward a story that began long before you.

You don't have to trace the past to honor it. You only have to live in a way that does justice to everything that came before.

As I write these letters, I find myself wondering about the world you'll grow into. What choices will shape you? Which memories will you hold close, and which will fade with time? I don't have the answers, but I've left behind my questions—some are reflections, some are just quiet hopes. You'll find them throughout these letters, not as instructions but as open doors, inviting you to step through and explore what they mean for you.

I wonder, Isha, what places will shape you? Which memories will stay with you as you grow, and which will you leave behind? Home isn't always a place—it can be a person, a feeling, or even the stories we tell ourselves. Wherever you find it, may it always remind you of who you are and where you've come from.

Appā

The Boy Who Left Mangadu

Imagine a young boy, barely twelve, standing alone in the busy streets of Madras. The city was a far cry from the quiet village he called home. The mix of sights, sounds, and smells was overwhelming—a world much grander than he had ever imagined. The marvel of a steam engine puffing at the railway station, the honking of cars weaving through the chaos, street vendors shouting, peddling their wares, and the air reeked of fried street food and the salt from the sea breeze. It was intoxicating. It was terrifying. And it was his first taste of freedom.

That boy was your grandfather. His life in Mangadu was simple. His father had a small grocery store in the village. As a boy, your grandfather often managed the store on his own. He was very generous with credit to the customers and like most boys his age, he had picked up smoking. His brothers were no better, and they covered for each other. One particular day, news reached him that his father had uncovered his generosity and intended to punish him severely. Urged by his brothers, he stole some money from the store and boarded a bus out of the village. His destination? Madras, the capital city 150 kilometers away. He had no plan, no guidance—just the urge to escape and a vague sense of adventure.

He stopped along the way, indulging in his love for cinema and the freedom of the road. The freedom was a revelation, and he devoured it. By the time he reached Madras, he was left with just a few rupees. The city was not only unfamiliar but also unforgiving. He had no idea where to go, but he knew one thing— his elder brother had been to the capital city and had worked at a fast food eatery before returning home. He wanted to go to the same place his brother had worked, to stay in the hostel his brother had spoken so much about. But reality set in quickly—he realized the people weren't as welcoming as he had hoped. He was told there was no job for him, and the hostel, the one his brother had described with such familiarity, had no place for him either. The doors he thought would be open were already shut. He drifted from cinema houses to parks, from bustling markets to empty street corners. Marina Beach. The railway station. The city at night was unforgiving. When the noise faded, the loneliness pressed in, heavier than hunger. He would curl up in a corner or any safe spot he could find, his stomach growling with hunger, his mind filled with thoughts of the family he had left behind. In those moments, the weight of loneliness felt like it might crush him, and the fear of the unknown was overwhelming. The thought of going back home crossed his mind countless times, but even in his deepest despair, he found a reason to stay; he discovered a resilience within himself he never knew existed. Thus began the story of my father, your grandfather. He found work at a small eatery, chopping vegetables and washing dishes in exchange for food and a corner to sleep. The work was tough, his young body aching from the long hours and the relentless demands of the kitchen, but he learned quickly. People were unforgiving, offering no break even though he was only 12, and his small stature made him look even younger. Yet, he never complained, knowing he was learning a skill. The eatery became more than a workplace; it became his lifeline, a place where survival and purpose met. During these physically exhausting days, he found himself reflecting on his family and upbringing and, for the very first time, felt thankful for the life he had so far.

The little eatery turned out to be a game-changer. It wasn't fancy—mostly packed with hardworking folks grabbing a quick bite—but it felt like a stroke of luck to him. The spot couldn't have been better, nestled near Fort St. George, Marina Beach, the Central railway station, and a string of cinema houses. Suddenly, he found himself in the middle of Madras' beating heart, soaking up its lively culture. For the first time, he felt himself falling for the city.

Weeks turned into months. Then a year. The city hardened him, shaped him. My father had adapted to the city as his home. Thoughts of Mangadu and his family were just occasional memories, fading into the background as he embraced this new life. He was clear that city life was for him. The city's vibrant culture captured his imagination, especially the glittering world of cinema.

The Dravidian Movement and the local political scene, advocating for a separate state for Tamils and a break from Congress representation, were on the rise. There were rallies and speeches led by the Dravidar Kazhagam, and by virtue of where he worked, he was always surrounded by conversations about the Movement and the need for a voice for the Tamils. But politics didn't interest him. While his friends were drawn into its fervor, my father remained indifferent. He didn't care who ruled—he was too busy surviving.

The cinema is what captured his attention. Every paisa he saved went to the theaters. He didn't just watch—he disappeared into those stories. For a few hours, the city, the hardship, the loneliness—it all faded into the flickering silver light.

Over time, he began to watch Hindi and English films as well. Through cinema, he picked up enough Hindi and English to hold conversations. This new skill didn't sit well with his friends, who were against the imposition of Hindi in their state. But this skill later opened the door for him, landing him a well-paying job at the newly established Madras Dental College canteen, where he met students from all over the country—a sliding door moment that changed his life.

Being young, relatable, and now a handsome man who could cook and share a love for smoking, the college students took him under their wing. They introduced him to new facets of life in Madras. They taught him to dress fashionably, navigate the city's social circles, and use grooming products to enhance his good looks. They also introduced him to football, and he began following the Mohun Bagan football team, a passion that lasted most of his life until cricket took over in his later years.

His quick wit and infectious smile drew people to him, and he soon found himself climbing the social ladder, mingling with a more sophisticated crowd. His flirtatious charm won him many admirers, and he thrived on the attention.

By now, he had started sending letters to his parents and had visits from his brothers and cousins, who tried to convince him to return to the village. However, these visitors seemed more interested in sightseeing than in earnestly persuading him to come back. Their half-hearted attempts at convincing him were easy to dismiss. But he wasn't in any mood to go back to his old life. He envisioned himself living in a big city with all its comforts and refinement and wanted to marry a culturally elite, educated, and polished woman. He wanted to build a family that would be the envy of all. To his credit, he had the skills and was earning good money compared to his peers. This vision sustained him through the long hours and lonely nights, a beacon of hope that guided him through the darkest times.

Life has its own ways of putting one in places and circumstances that test one's resolve. The exuberance of youth often forgets the trials of the generations before it. Young men seldom give due credit to their elders, driven by the urgency to carve their own path and the notion that they are creating something new, forgetting that it has all been done before and life is just a circle that repeats.

One late afternoon, while ambling around the port under a soft, hazy sky, his mind wandered back to the stories his father used to tell. Tales of working at the Madras port decades ago came rushing in, vivid and alive. His father had once recounted the tension of the week before the Japanese threatened to bomb the port during World War II—a moment so fraught it pushed the family back to Mangadu. For the first time, standing there by the docks, he felt the weight of those memories. It hit him that his father had walked this ground long before he had, navigating a world just as uncertain, just as pivotal. He had always thought of himself as the trailblazer, but this moment felt like a quiet reckoning, a realization that he was walking a path paved, in part, by his father's resilience.

This reflection hit him deeply. With this thought weighing on his heart, he decided to visit his family.

2.

Life has a way of disrupting even the best-laid plans. When he visited his village, he did so with the fanfare of a celebrity coming to town. He was decked out in the latest fashion and grooming, which made him stand out next to the sunburnt villagers. His arrival coincided with a severe drought that had gripped Tamil Nadu in the 1950s, leaving the people weak and miserable. It is always the villages that feel the brunt of any calamity; the cities bear the impact much later.

The contrast was stark; he looked fuller and healthier compared to the gaunt faces of the villagers. His well-fed appearance and stylish attire stood in sharp contrast to the weary, undernourished villagers who had been battling the relentless drought. The landscape was parched, the once fertile fields now barren, and the villagers' spirits as dry as the cracked earth beneath their feet.

He felt at home for the first time in years. After living alone for nearly five years, the familiar sights and sounds of his childhood house brought unexpected comfort. He found himself relaxing into old routines, enjoying meals with his family, and sharing stories of his time away.

His parents noticed this change. They seized the opportunity to arrange a marriage for him. They hoped that a wife would ground him and anchor him to his roots and the traditions of his community. He was matched with a young girl, probably 14, who had never left the village and had no clue that the earth revolved around the sun.

He was torn between his dreams and his duty to his family. Unable to refuse, he reluctantly agreed. It wasn't what he wanted, but he couldn't bring himself to refuse his family, a decision that would haunt him for years to come. It marked the beginning of a long struggle between his dreams and his obligations, a regret that would follow him throughout his life.

He was never the same again.

3.

Life gave him another chance when he was around 35. By then, he had moved to Bangalore for a better job, leaving his growing family of four children behind in Mangadu.

In Bangalore, he began carving out a place for himself and thriving in social circles. It was during this period that he met a young woman who would become an integral part of his story. She was very charming and had a city vibe. He fell in love. For the first time, he felt truly seen; it wasn't about his family or his charm—it was about a woman who understood him, one he could finally be with. He was in love. He had never been with anyone like her before, and this one felt real. Falling in love with her was like discovering a new world. He was captivated by her charm, intelligence, and the way she moved through life with confidence.

Their romance unfolded with a mature intensity that felt almost overwhelming for my father—walking through Bangalore's vibrant streets and exploring the city's local markets, street food, and beautiful gardens that the city was known for. In her, he found a kindred spirit who understood his aspirations and reignited an enthusiasm for life he thought had died long ago.

He found himself pulled in a different direction as he weighed the cost of his obligations against the possibility of true happiness. He dreamt of a life where he could be free from the burdens that had tied him down for so long. The pull of this new love was strong, filling him with a hope he hadn't felt in years.

He convinced himself he deserved this chance at happiness, even if it meant living a double life.

He married her without telling her anything about the four children he had left behind. She accepted his frequent absences when he visited Mangadu, perhaps choosing not to ask. Bigamy wasn't rare back then, but it was illegal. Though his friends and colleagues knew about his second wife, they never spoke of it aloud. It was all kept discreet as it wasn't permitted for anyone to hold a government job. A man with two lives. But he didn't care. He wanted what he had given up back. I am not sure how he managed it but somehow balanced this precarious situation.

4.

For three-odd years, he revelled in the joy and excitement of his newfound love and family. They laughed, made plans for the future, and enjoyed each other's company in ways he had never experienced before. They had two children, both boys, and it finally felt like he was living the life he was meant to live. But reality has a way of catching up, and soon, the cracks began to show.

The weight of his past, the family he left behind, and the guilt of his decisions started to haunt him. At first, he convinced himself that he could live two lives, compartmentalizing the joy of his new family from the responsibilities he had abandoned. But as time went on, the cracks in his facade grew wider. The birth of his second son brought everything to the surface. The joy of holding his newborn was eclipsed by the crushing realization of the life he had left behind. Every fond memory of his new family was shadowed by thoughts of the family he had betrayed.

He began to wonder if he was building his happiness on a foundation of lies—a fragile structure that could collapse with a single confession. The brief moments of happiness were overshadowed by the nagging responsibilities he couldn't escape. Ultimately, he realized that he couldn't run from his past forever. The dreams he had nurtured, the love he had found—it all came at a cost. And in trying to reclaim what he had given up, he found himself entangled in a web of consequences that he couldn't ignore.

Life, as it often does, dragged him back to reality, and secrets have a way of unraveling. The double life became too much to bear. He confessed, hoping that he could somehow manage the fallout. He admitted to his second wife that he had four children from his first marriage. The weight of his revelation was too much for her, and she asked him to leave.

Broken and filled with guilt, he returned to Mangadu. My mother, who had done everything to have him back in her life and had fought for it, accepted him. I was born out of that acceptance. I was the reconciliation child.

But my mother never forgot or forgave my father completely. My father was never the same again. He lived a life resigned to destiny and was distant.

5.

Isha, my darling daughter, I don't tell you this to judge your grandfather. I tell you this because choices shape generations. Some decisions follow you forever. Your grandfather's journey is a testament to the power of resilience and the importance of staying true to oneself. He pursued his dreams with fierce determination, even in the face of overwhelming odds. And then he gave up on them to make others happy.

As you navigate your own path, remember to respect everyone, from the porters to the waiters, from chefs to the taxi drivers. They all have dreams and aspirations, just like you. Every person carries their own dreams and struggles, just as your grandfather once did. Your grandfather was once a boy on the street, and he found the strength within himself to rise above his circumstances. Take courage from his story and understand that you come from a family that has fought helplessness and destitution to move toward growth. Pursue your life the way you want, but remember that when you make mistakes, own up to them and be willing to face the consequences. You are here for nobody but yourself. Go after your goals and learn from your grandfather's experiences. Giving up your dreams to keep others happy will only lead to regret. Life is too short to live by others' expectations. Embrace your ambitions with passion and courage. Be honest with yourself and those around you. Understand that your happiness and fulfillment are yours to claim. In this way, you will honor your grandfather's legacy, not by repeating his mistakes, but by forging your own path with integrity and determination.

I wish my father had pursued his passion and not given in to his family. I am sure I wouldn't have been here, but it wouldn't have mattered. He would have had a much happier life.

In the words of Charles Bukowski, a major influence in my life and writing:

"If you're going to try, go all the way. Otherwise, don't even start. This could mean losing girlfriends, wives, relatives, and maybe even your mind. It could mean not eating for three or four days. It could mean freezing on a park bench. It could mean jail. It could mean derision. It could mean mockery or isolation. Isolation is a gift. All the others are a test of your endurance, of how much you really want to do it. And you'll do it despite rejection and the worst odds. And it will be better than anything else you can imagine. If you're going to try, go all the way. There is no other feeling like that. You will be alone with the gods, and the nights will flame with fire. You will ride life straight to perfect laughter. It's the only good fight there is."

Your grandfather was just a boy when he stood on the streets of Madras, staring at a future unknown to him. He had no plan, no direction—only the belief that something bigger was waiting for him. Some choices follow us forever. Some doors close, and others open. We don't always know which decisions will shape our lives, but we have to choose anyway.

Isha, there will be moments when you feel the weight of choice pressing against you—when the world asks you to pick between the life expected of you and the life calling to you. It won't always be easy to know which to follow. I wonder, when that moment comes, will you choose the comfort of what's familiar, or will you step into the unknown, trusting that something bigger is waiting for you, just as it was for your grandfather? Appā.

Strength of Our Women

Here's another valuable story I would like to share with you…

My Nana passed away ten months after my father died. She broke her hip bone trying to negotiate a step into the house. She was in her nineties and the eldest member on my maternal side. For four days, she endured the pain without a word, brushing it off before it became evident that she was in serious trouble.

I was in India then, having moved back to spend time with my mother after my father's passing. We rushed her to the hospital. I sat next to the driver in the ambulance as he navigated through the crowded streets of Bangalore. It was humbling to see people making way for the ambulance and trust in humanity restored. My sisters were in the back, comforting her.

The doctors gave her a slim chance of survival, considering her age, but decided to go ahead with the surgery. I signed the waiver form for her operation, breaking it down as I did it. I had asked my sisters to do it, but they were already grieving. As they wheeled her toward the operating table, I held her hand and whispered my apologies, asking for forgiveness if I had ever hurt her. She just held on tighter. She was scared; I could see it in her eyes. She looked at me with longing and fear, wishing I could take her back home. Then they took her inside. She passed away 30 minutes later.

I cried for all she had done for our family through its darkest days. She had given us hope, courage, and assurance when we needed it the most, especially when the family was broken. She was once the thread that held us as a family together.

It was during my travels through Tamil Nadu, piecing together fragments of our family's history, that I began to truly understand Nana's life and all she had endured. Perhaps, had I not learned about her past, I might have grieved differently—less profoundly, less personally. But knowing the depth of her contributions, I mourned not just her loss but the immense void left behind by someone who had given so much of herself for us.

2.

To understand what her passing meant to the family, we must journey back to a different era: 1920s British India, Sriperumbudur, a small town 40 kilometers from Madras city. A place steeped in culture and tradition. Born into a well-to-do family, she married a bit late for her time, in her twenties, and had two daughters late as well. Within a few years of the birth of her second daughter, my mother, tragedy struck when her husband passed away.

By all accounts, her husband was a lazy man who adored his wife but never stood up for himself. She managed the affairs at home, which was quite progressive for that era. But when her husband passed away, she became a widow with two young daughters, and it was expected of her to be confined to rigid societal norms of widowhood and not participate in any decision-making. She was subjugated and stripped of her rights over her husband's share in his family's assets and was expected to retreat into the background. But Nana wasn't one to disappear quietly.

She made the brave decision to take her two young daughters and leave. She headed out for her ancestral village, close to Sunderamoodu, 60 kilometers away. This decision may sound normal and fitting today, but consider it in the context of early 19th-century South India. It was revolutionary for her time. There were no buses or cars, not even paved roads. She walked the distance with her two young daughters, with only a bullock cart carrying some essentials behind her. She never owned a pair of sandals in her life, and every step she took was on the bare, unforgiving ground. The paths were likely rough and uneven, fraught with the dangers of highway robbers and the elements, with nothing but sheer determination to drive her forward.

She once told me how the ground burned like fire beneath her feet, how it rose and blurred the horizon. She shielded her daughters with a thin sheet over them, placed them on the cart, and walked barefoot beside them. My mother, the youngest daughter, just over six years old, with no real understanding of what was happening, wanted to hold her hand and walk alongside. At times, the sight of her daughters made her think of giving up, but then it would have condemned them to the same fate she had fought so hard to escape. She wasn't ready to accept it.

They often took shelter under a banyan tree or punga maram (beech tree), where they would rest, sharing parboiled tamarind rice and buttermilk. She recalled that if her daughters had not been so cooperative, she would have given up her sense of self-respect and returned to her in-laws' house and faded away. But she knew they would not receive any self-respect, and surrendering her daughters to the same subjugation was unthinkable.

Imagine the kind of strength it takes to walk into the unknown with nothing but your children and your will. She didn't know if there would be shelter at the end of the road, a warm meal, or even kindness. But she walked anyway. We can only imagine what must have gone through that woman's mind and how strong her resolve must have been to subject herself and her children to such uncertainty. She knew she was going to her parents' house, and that confidence alone kept her going. And she wasn't disappointed. Her brothers welcomed her warmly. They gave her a piece of farmland purchased for 53 rupees and let her manage it. With that piece of land, she built a life—a bold, independent single mother, a widow, living all by herself with two daughters in a society still entrenched in taboo.

3.

Reflecting on my 30-year-old nana making that trip, I am humbled by her incredible resolve and physical strength. She had to bear not just the physical burden but also the emotional weight of leaving behind the remnants of her old life, moving forward with only dreams and hopes to guide her. With every step, she defied societal norms that dictated a widow should live a life of confinement and dependence. She had nothing to lose, and with her children by her side, she started a new life.

This profound act of rebellion against the prescribed roles and limitations placed on women of her time alienated her from society. She faced obstacles: the cultural stigma of being a widow, the challenges of single-handedly raising two young children, and the societal expectations that sought to bind her to a life of subservience.

She had to navigate a society that was often harsh and unforgiving to women, especially widows. Widows in her era were expected to live in seclusion; their lives were fraught with challenges. Widows were often marginalized, denied inheritance rights, and subjected to demeaning traditions and rituals designed to strip them of their dignity and autonomy. Many were forced into economic hardship, finding themselves dependent on charity or low-paying labor, with some even pushed into begging or prostitution to survive.

4.

It was a time when India was still under British rule, and the presence of the colonizers was felt even in the remote corners of the country. Your grandmother once recounted a story from her childhood that reflects the fear and uncertainty of those times. A British army officer stationed in the nearby town of Arcot had fallen from his horse and was resting under a tree. He spotted your grandmother, then just a little girl, and asked her to fetch help. Terrified by the sight of a white man, she ran back to the village, screaming that a 'vellai durai' (white officer) had come to capture them. Her cries and the sight of soldiers in the village coming to take the officer back to the fort sent the entire village into a panic that lasted for days. It was a reflection of the times and the broader uncertainties and tensions of a nation under colonial rule.

My mother's cry and the panic may sound like an exaggeration today, but it reflected a deep-seated fear of colonial rule—of stories that the land holds in its psyche that may take some generations to heal.

The story is of the 'Vellai Durai,' a broad term for pale outsiders who ruled over the locals. These men who came with soldiers and, in the past, had taken our people away. Young men disappeared from villages, never to return. Families lived for generations without fathers, brothers, or sons. These men, we learned later, were sent far across the seas. South Africa. Malaysia. Mauritius. Some even ended up in Fiji and the West Indies.

But it wasn't just the men. Married women without children and young girls were taken. They became 'Ayahs'—maids and nannies in British homes across India. Some came back years later, too old to work or released by officers returning to England. They brought back stories—some of kindness, many of hardship.

5.

My nana preferred the British ruling the land over the locals. She had been let down by the locals, her tradition, and her family, and it seemed to her that the British, through their brute presence, could humble the so-called upholders of values in society. She found vicarious satisfaction in seeing the locals humbled, even though it was at the hands of a colonial foreign power.

This stand came from the humiliation she faced in society as a single mother. During the festival of harvest, Pongal, she was once publicly chastised by a local elder for participating in the celebrations. Widows were expected to live in seclusion, but being asked to leave in front of her daughters left her broken. Yet, even in her pain, she refused to submit. She stood her ground and let her daughters enjoy the colors, bullock races, and stage theatre that is usually put on during the three days of festivities.

Some shunned her. Some admired her. But no one forgot the widow who refused to fade into silence. It didn't stop there. She wanted to give her two daughters a platform to aspire to more than just marriage. Despite societal norms of the time, which didn't support and believe in the merits of educating a girl child, she understood the importance of education and sent her daughters to school.

However, for your grandmother, my mother, the school experience was very short. After just two days, both daughters kept coming back home in tears, refusing to go back. My nana, understanding their distress, allowed them to stay home and assist with the household and work in the paddy fields. Though education was not their path, she still instilled in them a sense of self-worth and resilience.

6.

Growing up, the sisters found joy in the simplest of things. They spent their days playing in the fields, chasing after goats, and helping their mother with household chores. Every evening, after a long day in the fields, my nana would light a small oil lamp at the household altar. She would gather her daughters and recount the day or share a story about ancestors or mythology. These moments of quiet reflection were her way of instilling a sense of hope and courage to see through the rough patch. Her unwavering faith, even in the face of adversity, became a cornerstone of their upbringing.

The air was always filled with the scent of jasmine, and the sounds of village life—children laughing, cattle settling in for sleep, the distant chime of temple bells—created a comforting and familiar rhythm. In these moments, amidst the struggles, they found fragments of peace and normalcy.

The girls grew into young women, taking on more responsibilities at home and in the fields. It was during this time that a young man from Madras arrived with an air of confidence. My mother, just 14 years old, married him at her mother's insistence. But the joy didn't last. My mother found herself back at her mother's doorstep with four children, broken and seeking refuge. Her husband had left to find work in the city. At first, there were promises of support. Then the visits grew sparse. Then the money stopped. And then, one day, he simply never returned, leaving her to shoulder the burden alone.

Nana took it upon herself to fight the battle again, this time not for herself but for her daughter and grandchildren. She stood by my mother's side as her four grandchildren clamored for attention, nourishment, and shelter. The pain of longing and the weight of responsibility were immense, but she didn't waver. Both Nana and my mother refused to let the circumstances break them.

While Nana took care of the kids and the household, your grandmother toiled in the fields, worked in brick kilns, and laid roads to keep the money coming.

In the end, perseverance prevailed. My father returned, and the family was united. Nana's assurance and unwavering support made this reconciliation possible.

7.

Life, however, tends to resolve one aspect only to open another, testing our resolve and preparing us for higher things. Soon after, she received the devastating news that her eldest daughter had passed away, leaving behind a grown-up son and a young daughter. The son managed well, but the daughter suffered from chronic epilepsy. With no foreseeable cure, the family treated her like an outcast, akin to a leper. Her condition was misunderstood and feared; she was often tied to a pole, and food was left out at the door in a bowl.

Despite living miles away, my nana never abandoned her granddaughter. Every second day, she came—feeding her, washing her, combing her hair, speaking softly where others only feared. Her care transcended the limitations imposed by fear and ignorance. She did this for 14 years. Then, one night, her granddaughter passed in her sleep. The loss shattered her. But in time, she found solace in knowing the girl no longer had to suffer.

During our summer holidays, when we stayed at Nana's house, she would take us along. I remember being scared of my cousin back then. Reflecting on it now, I feel a sense of embarrassment at how I behaved and treated my cousin, and it also fills me with immense pride for the kind of woman my grandmother was.

Nana's life was marked by cycles of loss and perseverance; each struggle met with quiet dignity and unyielding resolve.

8.

Isha, as I share these stories with you, I marvel at how different your grandmother's childhood was from your own. Growing up in a world of technology and instant communication, your challenges are vastly different from those of the little girl who ran through the fields of Pudur.

Isha, the same fire that burned in your Nana lives in you. Her strength, her defiance, her resilience—it's in your bones, your blood, your very being. You are part of a line of women who refused to be silenced. Never forget that. If you ever feel overwhelmed, think of all the women who came before you—your Nana's walk to Pudur, your grandmother's resolve to work the fields. None of them knew what tomorrow would bring, but they never gave up.

I wonder, Isha, when the world asks you to shrink, will you choose silence, or will you stand your ground? And when life challenges you, will you remember the fire that runs in your blood, passed down through women who refused to disappear?

With the opportunities you have today come responsibilities. Use your voice. Use your strength. Let your presence be a testament to the women who paved the way, and let their spirit carry you forward.

Your presence here is a tribute to all the women who paved the way. With the opportunities you have today come responsibilities. Use your voice to speak out against injustice, your strength to support those in need, and your compassion to make the world a better place. Stand tall in the face of adversity, and never forget that you carry the legacy of extraordinary women whose spirits live on in you.

Your Appā

What My Father Taught Me

Your grandfather was a handsome man. He didn't aspire to much and lived a simple life. He didn't leave behind grand achievements, but he left behind a life. He had a routine, and he stuck to it; it suited him, but it was harder for my mother, who managed our home and four kids. She never complained; she knew her role, and he also knew that she ran the house, and he never interfered with her decisions.

His day began early. He was out of the door ten minutes before six every morning, lit a cigarette on his walk to work, which he stubbed out on a wall next to the time office where he stamped his card. At two in the afternoon, he would come out of the same time office, light another cigarette on his way home, stub it out on the wall near our house door, change, and get on his bike. We wouldn't see him until after dinner. His nighttime routine was equally predictable: a smoke while sitting on his bed before sleep. It wasn't that he was absent from our lives; he provided for us and was there when needed; he kept a part of himself apart as if he belonged to a different world that felt a bit distant.

2.

As years went by, his health began to fade. I noticed he moved a bit slower, his once firm grip softened, and his cough from years of smoking became more frequent. I used to visit India every year, even if it was just for a week, to see him and the family. I remember vividly the last time he walked up to the house gate to send me off. I saw him struggle; his steps were labored, but he still managed; he waved and told me to look after myself. That was our final conversation.

I didn't get a chance to speak to him at the end of his life; he couldn't speak. They had cut his chest open and had tubes running out of his throat and mouth. He hadn't eaten a meal for over a fortnight and was going through medications to manage the side effects. The discomfort from weakened lungs had now been overtaken by complications caused by the heavy-duty trial medicines.

When his health declined sharply, and he was under intensive care, my sister called to inform me that he was struggling. I was in Melbourne. "He's unwell," she said, though she assured me he wasn't critical and stressed there was no need for me to come back home. She mentioned 'home'. I paused, turning the word over in my mind. I'd been away for a decade now and had built a new life in a different city. Though by now we were calling different cities and places home, in our family psyche, home was always his house. It wasn't a structure; it was a feeling anchored in his presence. It was intrinsic.

My sister's call was a reach out—as families do because it is the right thing to do. It was a gentle pull, a reminder of my place in the family. She still hoped that he would recover and remain our father, but I had a feeling he was leaving us. Within hours, I was on a plane to Bangalore, arriving at the family door the next morning.

When I arrived, my long hair and absence for over a year made me unrecognizable to my sister, and when she finally did, unprepared for my arrival, she didn't rush to greet me. She rushed inside instead to compose herself and wash away her gushing tears. The strength she'd held onto finally was crumbling. She had been holding it together for the family until then, and now, with my presence at the door, she knew it was no time for denial anymore and let down her guard.

Two weeks later, my father passed away in his bed, surrounded by my mother and his children.

A couple of days ago, India won a cricket Test match in Perth—a sport he loved. My elder brother sat beside him, sharing the news while he slept. My father barely had the strength to react. His breathing was shallow, his face calm but distant. I think he liked hearing it, even if he couldn't smile. He followed the game very fondly. There was always cricket or a movie playing on TV, filling the quiet of his room.

We had brought him home to die in his bed, as the doctors had given up. His eyes still had the strength to look at his family, but his breathing was shallow. He knew he had been leaving many weeks ago and had made peace with that.

I was lying next to him that night, my face close to his, holding his hands the whole time, feeling his faint pulse under my fingers. I had been awake most of the night, just touching him, hoping he would somehow make it for a few more days.

3.

Around eight that morning, his pulse weakened. I called everyone. The room quickly filled up with familiar faces and distant cousins. There was silence. No whispers. No inquiries. Just silence.

My elder brother sat beside him. He broke the unspoken silence code, and whispered, "Is he still alive?"

I felt the faint beat beneath my fingers and nodded. And then shortly after, just like that, the pulse disappeared.

My trembling hands still holding his, searching desperately for any trace of life. Tears rolled down my face as I looked up at my mother. She saw my tears and began to wail. My brothers and sisters joined in, their cries filling the room as each one sat beside him, speaking their goodbyes, clinging to the hope he might still hear.

I was still holding his hands. I couldn't let go. In that moment, it felt as though letting go would mean losing him entirely. I was trying to hold on to his presence, anything, just a moment longer.

4.

My father had nearly died once before. Almost. That's what we think. I was nine years old. He often woke early, smoking and talking to my seemingly asleep mother, who responded with closed eyes—a mystery to me. It was a lifelong routine they had, and I'm certain it had been happening well before I arrived.

I woke up to my mother's frantic cries. My father lay still, his cigarette still smoldering on the pillow. All efforts to wake him failed, and there was loud wailing from my mother. I had never seen her like that before, nor had I heard her cry so loudly. I slapped his face and checked his breathing, but there was no response.

How ironic it feels now, decades later, that life would place me on his deathbed once again, checking for his breathing and heartbeat.

My mother was now seated right behind him, shaking him and looking at me with helpless eyes, tears rolling down her cheeks. After 30 seconds of panic, he opened his eyes. He seemed surprised at the commotion. He was more annoyed that his cigarette had burnt the pillow. He glanced at my mother, more apologetic that he had damaged the pillow than by what had transpired. He got up, changed, and went to work shortly after that. The same man: no goodbyes, no good mornings. Just out the door, lighting up a cigarette on his way to the time office.

He had no recollection of what had happened. It bewildered me.

That night, I overheard him telling my mother his greatest fear of leaving us with nothing. He knew what had happened that morning. I didn't understand it then—that his greatest fear was leaving us with nothing. It took me years to fully grasp how deeply that fear shaped his actions. His worry was genuine, and our lives would have changed if he'd died then.

He passed away 22 years later. By then, we had done enough for him to believe that we would survive without him. The years had also given him time for some introspection and soul-searching to make peace with his death and mortality.

5.

A chef by trade, my father started as a kitchen hand at 13 and rose to become a chef-de-partie by the time he retired. His lack of English limited his advancement. Twice, he declined promotions, insecure about conversing with higher-ups. This insecurity stayed with him throughout his life and largely influenced us. Though literate in Tamil, he confined his reading to bi-weeklies and gossip and didn't go beyond that. He didn't need to and wasn't going to expend himself to go beyond.

My love for cooking stems from him. When choosing a career, I wanted to follow him into the kitchen and join him as an apprentice. I worked as one for almost three months until he insisted I join the service side of the hotel. He couldn't bear to see me spending hours on end standing next to an open fire stove and wok.

When I persisted, he urged me to focus on my studies. A sliding door moment—a gentle nudge that shaped the course of my life.

Looking back, I can see how that moment, that gentle push was love. It was my father's way of steering me toward something bigger, even if I couldn't see it then. It couldn't have been easy for him to steer me away from the path he had walked, to encourage me to venture beyond the familiar and into the unknown. But he did it because he believed in me and wanted the best for me. That moment set me on a journey I never would have imagined, but one I remain grateful for.

When he retired, he felt a big part of who he was taken away. His routine, his purpose—gone. He now felt stripped, leaving him lost and withdrawn, tethered to the television. His lifelong smoking habit now caused him pain. Losing physical strength and mobility, he felt defeated despite our love and respect.

My mother didn't make it any easier for him. She kept prompting him to find work, her taunts often laced with remarks about his younger years of abandonment. It was as though she was reclaiming her voice, taking back the power she'd once held in silence. She reminded him, often bitterly, that he was now living off the family he had once left behind. These words cut deeply, and though he rarely retaliated, they left him visibly diminished. He was half the person he had been earlier, keeping to himself in moments where once he would have stood tall.

Still, he managed to get a few assignments, all from his former students who now had businesses of their own and respected him deeply. He confided in me once that he took those assignments not for the money but simply to be out of the house and away from my mother's sharp remarks. "It's quieter there," he said, and the sadness in his voice stayed with me.

But I don't blame her. I probably would have done the same, or worse, if I were in her position. The anger she carried—the frustration and hurt from years of managing the household alone, of accepting and forgiving—was human. It was a reflection of the sacrifices she had made and the toll those years had taken on her. She had given up so much to keep the family together, and perhaps those words were her way of reclaiming some of the power she had lost along the way.

My father understood this. He accepted her anger without argument, without confrontation. He carried it quietly, knowing it was part of the cost of their shared history. It was heartbreaking to see him reduced to this—to witness a man who had once been a source of quiet strength now struggling to maintain his dignity in the face of both external challenges and the echoes of his past.

As his body began failing and he could no longer walk more than 10 meters without stopping, relying heavily on inhalers just to breathe, he felt a profound sense of betrayal– he felt betrayed that his past efforts had not been adequately rewarded and time was slipping away. His self-worth plummeted, seeing himself as a dependent rather than the head of the family, which deeply hurt him.

It was sad to watch him become this. He had found his place in the world, provided us all with an education, and was caring and a good provider. He had somehow instilled in us the belief that we were here to leave a mark. Yet, he judged himself by different standards and considered his achievements to be minimal.

Like Homer Simpson in the 'Do It for Her' episode of The Simpsons, he probably gave up on his dreams, setting aside any urge to chase grand ambitions. Instead, he focused on his steady, low-paying job, finding comfort in its reliability—knowing it would always provide for his family, even if just enough.

When it finally came time for him to live for himself, it was too late—his body was already failing.

Amid his struggles with retirement, the arrival of his grandchildren brought a new light into his life. It was as if, in their innocent eyes and joyful laughter, he had found a renewed sense of purpose and meaning. He devoted his life, after that, to them. He now had a routine responsibility and took it very seriously.

Perhaps it was the realization of his own mortality, or perhaps it was the joy he found in his grandchildren, but he seemed determined to make up for the time he had lost with us, his own children.

In his final days, he was a man at peace, having shed his guilt and remorse. He accepted who he was and what he had done, confident in our future; he had made his peace with himself, with the world, and with death. I am not sure I can say that of many people.

6.

After his passing, the realization that I would never again hear his voice or see his smile was a weight that settled heavily on my heart. There was also a sense of guilt, a nagging feeling that I hadn't done enough, hadn't been present enough in his final years. The distance between us, both physical and emotional, seemed suddenly vast and insurmountable.

I replayed old conversations, wondering if I could have said or done something differently, something that would have brought us closer together. Regret is a slow, steady ache, isn't it? It doesn't scream—it whispers, replaying moments you can't get back.

In the days and weeks that followed, as I navigated the strange new landscape of life without my father, I found myself grappling with a mix of emotions. There were moments of deep sadness when a memory would surface unexpectedly and bring with it a fresh wave of tears. But there were also moments of laughter, shared stories, and fond recollections that brought us closer together as a family.

Through it all, I couldn't shake the feeling that my father's passing had fundamentally changed me in some way. It was as if a veil had been lifted, revealing the fragility and preciousness of life in a way I had never fully understood before. Losing him was a reminder that life is a series of fleeting moments, each more fragile than we realize.

I found myself reevaluating my priorities, questioning the things I had once taken for granted. I submitted my resignation and took off to India to spend some time with my mother—hoping to grieve in my own way and reconnect with the threads of our family story. It felt like the only way to make sense of what had been lost.

7.

But as the days unfolded, I realized it wasn't just about grieving—in the time I was spending at home with her, it became a process of knowing my mother as a person—the woman who had been the constant thread in our family's story.

In those months, I began to see her in a new light. Her quiet strength, her sacrifices, and her unwavering love for a man who wasn't always easy to love became clearer. I realized how much she had carried silently, her resilience shaping the foundation of our family.

During that time, I also traveled to retrace my father's footsteps as a young man. It was a journey into his past and, through it, into the roots of our family's story. Walking through the places he lived and worked and speaking with people who remembered him, I began to piece together parts of his life that had always felt just out of reach.

Through these moments, I uncovered truths about both sides of my family—their struggles, choices, and quiet victories. Each story I learned helped me better understand how their lives shaped my own. These memories, both shared and uncovered, are what I am passing on to you, Isha. They are not just about your grandfather or grandmother—they are about us all, about how understanding were those who came before us.

8.

Years later, now almost fifty with my own children, I am able to understand him and his regrets. My father's journey in his later years taught me something invaluable: life rarely follows a script, and neither do we. He lived through disappointments and unfulfilled dreams, yet he found a way to redefine his purpose and embrace what life offered him in those moments. His strength came not from grand achievements but from the quiet resilience of showing up for his family, even when the world around him changed. Despite the hardships, he made peace with himself, accepting his journey and its limitations.

My father's story reminds me that life is unpredictable—it will challenge your plans, diminish your prominence, and shift the world you once knew. You won't always have control, and that's okay. My father's story is a reminder that it's not about holding onto certainty but about adapting with grace and finding strength in the connections and love that ground you.

Isha, life doesn't always follow the path we expect. Some dreams shift, some doors close, and some choices stay with us forever. But through it all, what truly defines us is how we carry ourselves through the unexpected.

I wonder, Isha, what will guide you when life takes you down a road you never planned to walk? Will you fight to shape it into something meaningful? Will you trust that even in uncertainty, there is strength to be found?

My father's greatest lesson wasn't in what he built—it was in how he kept moving forward, even when life didn't go as planned. That's what I hope you carry with you, Isha—not a map, but the resilience to keep going, no matter where the path leads.

The legacy I hope you carry forward is about embracing who you are—flaws, struggles, and all. Find meaning in the relationships and values that shape your journey. That's what my father left me, and that's what I hope to leave you: a sense of strength rooted in authenticity and a reminder that even in the face of life's unpredictability, we endure, we love, and we continue—carrying forward the stories and strength of those who came before us.

Isha, true strength lies in self-acceptance and the ability to adapt to life's changes.

As you navigate your own journey, take his story as a reminder:

1. Pursue your dreams, but don't lose sight of those who matter most.
2. Mistakes will happen—own them, learn from them, and keep moving forward.
3. Life isn't about control. Sometimes, you have to let go, adapt, and trust that you'll find your way.
4. Success isn't defined by others' expectations. It's about being true to yourself.

My father taught me that. And I hope, through this story, he teaches you, too, my baby. Yours only, Appā.

My Early Days

As a boy, I imagined countless worlds where I could be anything I wanted to be, and I liked it that way. The reality of life had some pain, but I didn't see pain as pain back then; it was more that life hadn't given enough, hadn't given us a fair share; grief always followed me and, at times, showed up not as sorrow, but as disappointment. I was more angry at life than at my parents. I never blamed them. I won't say I never blamed; I did a fair share of it, but it was more to cover for my own shortcomings. We knew we were better sheltered than much of the humanity around us. The disappointment, though we didn't show more of it, was obvious from the outside. We didn't have much growing up. Sharing wasn't about caring; it was just about staying together adrift. With seven of us, my father did his best to keep his family safe. Anything else was a luxury.

We didn't have much to play with, no fancy toys with colored flashing lights, no superhero figurines, or bicycles with plastic baskets in the front; we were always on the sidelines and watched others show off their treasures. But it didn't bother me, the sidelines became stages for my dreams. I could imagine and be anyone I wanted to be. They were stages, battlefields, kingdoms. In my mind, I was anyone I wanted to be. I found that engaging and things around me interesting; the trees, animals, birds, and insects were all part of my game, my loyal playmates; rocks, sticks, flowers, and soil were my pretend toys, each one a treasure, a story, a friend. I would follow butterflies to high mountains, slay a thousand dragonflies with a wooden spoon, climb trees to rescue imaginary kingdoms, jump fences, sprint everywhere, hoot like superheroes, enact legends of any lore, and rise to be a savior in the end.

I faked sickness countless times to skip school; I didn't hate it, but it never taught me much; it was a luxury daycare at my father's expense. The school was just a backdrop; my real lessons came from the land, the sky, and the streets. By the time I was five, I had already been caught sneaking out of school thrice and even managed to come back home a few times unnoticed. I scored just enough to stay at school, and the teachers knew I had it in me to pull through life, and they just let me be.

Evenings were my favorite time of the day. I would lie on the roof with friends, tracking stars and spotting satellites; I would jump into dirty ponds to bring home fishes and keep them in pickle jars and watch them grow, each fish a silent companion in my solitary aquarium. Drinking a glass of milk at sunrise was enough to last till sunset, and when sunset finally arrived, I would curse it for not having enough to play but feeling grateful for the adventures it brought. I always found running barefoot under the Indian sun easy, not that buying a shoe was an option; I was alive and didn't have to worry how food came to the table or how much of it; all that mattered was our parents loved us all.

〰 〰 〰

In this theatre of growing up,
I have fallen from trees,
have had stones and broken glass cut and pierce my skin;
bruises were a daily event, but they weren't worth stopping life for;
have had wild bees chase and bite me,
and I still carry a scar,
I have jumped naked into water tanks to beat the summer heat,
girls and boys together, nudity didn't matter,
none of us lost innocence till very late,
and that innocence still remains,

am paying the price, not knowing betrayal exists,
have lied many times, white and black, blue and green lies,
not that the lies were to make else loose,
but just to have some more fun at the race of growing up. Days
when watching a snail in the backyard
meant more than failing at school,
days when rain meant dancing under it
and then the thrill of finding refuge anywhere,
a game in itself,
days when laughter came from deep within
days when, despite having nothing,
fear didn't cast a meaning onto us,
days when tomorrow didn't exist,
and there were days when poverty showed its dark shadows,
and there were days when people told us we were here to lose,
and it just gave us another reason to find this life more exciting.

〜 〜 〜

Back in my days, we had half a day of school on Saturdays. It was
a fun day to be at school, and I always looked forward to it. It was
a day of storytelling, learning moral science and civics, and ending
with an hour of painting. A lot of who I am today is because of
those Saturdays. I used to write for a small school magazine,
"Young Rhymes," which came out every term. Looking back,
though I believed I had great writing skills, the only reason that
my work was always published is mine had nothing to do with
school topics. I always looked forward to the publication coming
out, which was usually on a Saturday, and I would then take it
home and show it to my mother. I rejoiced greatly at showing her
what I had created and seeing my name in print.

But on one occasion, which also happened to be the last time I
contributed. I had written about a topic discussed in our Civics

class. The topic was Poverty. I had introspected what poverty meant, and I had suggested that poverty shouldn't just be seen as a metric of a country's wealth but also be looked at as the state of the mind of the people in poverty.

The Civics teacher, Miss Rani, asked me to read to the class what I had written, which I thought was rather unusual as she was very particular about how she managed her time. After my reading, she rebuked and mocked me in front of the class and asked me to just stick to the syllabus and failed me in Civics. This was very humiliating, as no one in the history of the school had failed in Civics, and she had failed me not for my ideas, but for my bad handwriting.

My humiliation became school gossip. For weeks, the taunts followed me. This was my first realization that writing your thoughts out for public consumption does come with critique, and it's always not palatable. The humiliation stayed with me, and for years, I stopped writing. It wasn't until college that I found my voice again.

I still believe poverty is more than lack of money—it's a state of mind. You can either accept it or reject it, but the responsibility for what you do in poverty still comes down to the individual. I propose that it be looked at as a vacuum that has been opened for the individual to fill up with anything. It could be filled with abundance, love, sharing, smiles, laughter, and a sense of contentment, or it could be filled with hatred, blame game, and denial.

And that's exactly what I did with my life. I never let poverty around me define me, and it also made it easier for me to step away from accumulating when I had the means to do so. I refuse to let possessions burden me. I step lightly around possessions. Don't let worldly possessions burden you.

Isha, life isn't about what you have but how you live. Don't let fear shadow your dreams. Embrace each day as I did—barefoot, curious, and unafraid of what lies ahead. Let your imagination guide you, and let your dreams carry you to a life of endless adventures. Remember, living lightly and freely is the greatest gift you can give yourself. Don't stack your life with so many commitments and obligations that there's no room left for your passion. Leave enough space in your life to drop everything and chase what truly matters.

I wonder, Isha, when life asks you to choose between comfort and adventure, will you be brave enough to leap? Will you trust that even in uncertainty, there's magic waiting to be found?

Love, Appā

Part 2: Love and Family

(commitment, connection, forgiveness)

Isha, love is not one thing. It is not just passion, nor is it just duty. It is complicated, layered, and sometimes unrecognizable in the moment. Love has been many things in my life—steady, uncertain, painful, and healing. I have questioned it, fought it, walked away from it, and held onto it when nothing else made sense.

In these letters, you'll find stories of love in all its forms—love that was chosen, love that was expected, love that endured even when it changed shape. Some of these stories may challenge how you see love. Some may feel familiar. And maybe, one day, you will look back at your own life and realize that love was present in places you never thought to look. Take what speaks to you, and let the rest find you in time.

How I Met Your Mother

Isha, I was born just three miles from where your mother was born, though many years apart. By the time I entered the world, she had already left, carried off to Koala Country as a baby, just six or seven months old. I didn't leave home until I was 24 years of age.

Our paths were different. Our childhoods couldn't have been more different. Even our dreams for the future were different. Our worlds were different—everything separated us. Your mother grew up traveling the world while I observed life unfold from my own small corner. She kept a journal carefully recording her expenses and her travels, while I told stories to anyone who'd listen and had little money. We shouldn't have met.

But destiny brought us together. Think about it, Isha—what are the chances that two people born just three miles apart, separated by years and continents, would find their way to one another? Sometimes, it feels as though the universe conspired to bring us together.

When the call came, I migrated to your mother's koala land. I didn't know then that just as I arrived, she was feeling the pull to leave—the place she had called home no longer enough to hold her. Life has its own mysterious ways of connecting people, surprising us with how perfectly it aligns stories, crossing paths we never imagined we would meet.

Your mother and I couldn't have been more different. She liked to collect stamps, flag pins, and postcards from every place she visited. I embraced my new life for its experiences and sunshine. Her personality was marked by thoughtful reflection and deliberate, intentional actions while I floated through life as a spirit.

It's strange to think of how we met. Some things are beyond our control. They simply unfold in time, surprising us with how perfectly they fit into our lives. I never thought I would find such a loving and caring partner, yet there she was—a blessing of sorts from the gods I worship.

2.

Time passed, and the days went by. I continued to live as a carefree spirit, happy in my solitude. Even the most content solitude can start to feel hollow. Being alone wasn't sad—it had been a gift, a time to know myself. But slowly, a quiet yearning crept in. Not for just anyone—for someone who would share my solitude, not disturb it. I longed for a partner who could share my solitude, who could understand me and enjoy my company.

A partner who would greet me with a cup of tea and evening snacks when I returned home from work—just like wives often do for their husbands in my hometown. Not really. They stopped doing that decades ago. I was looking for someone who shared my cultural values, beliefs, and traditions. I didn't have many expectations, just a few that could be met by a caring, loving woman.

And that woman turned out to be your mother.

3.

With a few clicks on the internet, I reached out to her. I didn't know then how much this decision would change my life.

Maybe your mother felt it too—that quiet longing for belonging. She saw me online, among many others, and decided to send me a short, clear email. No unnecessary words. No hesitation. The clarity in her words impressed me, and we arranged to meet. She listened as I told her stories, and I was full of it—literally. She spoke softly, shared her own stories, and talked about the people who were close to her. She desired adventures and had a list of places she wanted to see. She liked her eggs runny, and her company felt warm and pleasant.

There was something genuine about her, and I could tell she genuinely cared about people. She maintained bonds, no matter how small, and kept them alive.

Your mother showed a childlike delight whenever I told her I was coming to meet her. She would giggle and play with a strand of her hair, her eyes lighting up.

And in those moments, I knew. I wasn't alone anymore. She had already filled the empty spaces in my world with color, and I hadn't even noticed it happening. I had someone to care for me, someone truly special, someone I wanted to spend the rest of my life with.

And now, you are part of this circle. The story that began three miles apart, stretched across years and continents, now lives in you.

You are part of the story now. Our story.

Stay true to yours. Let it unfold in its own time, in its own way—beautiful, unexpected, and entirely yours.

And when love finds its way to you, ask yourself: Is this a person you invite into your solitude, not because you need them, but because you want them there?

Appā

The Day You Chose Me

Isha, my love, you were a miracle. Born against all odds, with the biological clock ticking relentlessly against us, your arrival defied logic and probabilities. Your journey began long before your first breath, in a moment etched in my memory.

I remember sitting in a fertility specialist's office, the polished wooden chair cool beneath me, a stark contrast to the warmth of your mother's hand gripping mine. The sterile white walls, blank and lifeless, seemed to close in on us, reflecting our fears and fragile hopes. The sharp smell of disinfectant in the air, a scent that would forever remind me of this pivotal moment.

Your mother sat beside me, her hands were cold and clammy in mine, her pulse racing against my palm as her fingers tightening as if holding on for dear life. She had poured herself into research in the weeks leading up to this appointment, her nights spent in the blue glow of her phone, skimming through forums and medical journals.

Now, as we waited, her eyes, usually so bright and full of life—the same rich brown that you would inherit—were clouded with worry. I watched as she silently mouthed prayers, her lips moving in a whispered litany of hope. The ticking of the clock on the wall seemed unnaturally loud, each second a reminder of the hope of a child slipping away from us.

The specialist finally spoke, and his words fell heavily in the quiet room, each syllable carving away at our hopes. He offered a slim chance of success, his voice matter-of-fact, clinical as if he were reading from a textbook rather than discussing the future we so desperately wanted to create.

The specialist was expecting us to drop the idea, his pen poised over his notepad, and suggested we consider other options—perhaps think about getting a dog instead.

Your mother's cry that day was like nothing I'd ever heard—a sound so raw and filled with anguish that it seemed to echo off the walls. It tore through me, leaving a permanent mark. It was a keening wail of grief, of dreams seemingly shattered, of a future suddenly uncertain. Even now, I sometimes hear it, a reminder of how deeply we longed for you.

But in her grief, I saw something change in her. Her eyes burned with a fierce determination. The tears stopped. She wiped her cheeks, squared her shoulders, and turned to the specialist. "We'll go ahead," she said, her voice steady and resolute. It was at that moment that I knew—we knew you were coming.

2.

What the specialist didn't know, what none of us could have imagined, was that you weren't coming alone. The IVF process was grueling—an endless cycle of hormone injections, mood swings, and countless clinic visits produced three embryos. There was you, the one who didn't make it and what I call your twin. The three of you floating together in that clinical dish.

I remember the first time we saw you all on the screen. Three tiny clusters of cells, each with the potential for human life. The image was grainy, black and white, but to us, it was the most beautiful sight in the world.

You were the one who came to us, Isha. You chose us. You chose to nestle in your mother's womb, growing and thriving. But I often think about the one who didn't have the strength to grow, and your twin embryo still suspended in time, still frozen. What you three would have been like? Would you have been identical or distinct opposites? Would you have shared a bond I could only hope to understand?

This other embryo, this shadow of what could have been, reminds me of the delicate balance of life. It's a reminder of how many stars had to align perfectly for you to be here, for us to hold you, love you, and call you ours.

3.

I knew you long before you existed. I knew you were coming years before your mother got pregnant. Your name lived in my thoughts before you did. Isha. Infinity. A ruling goddess. A goddess who was conceived well before any physical form had taken. Your name had become a lullaby in my thoughts. As your mother's belly swelled up with a promise of you, your presence grew in the quiet spaces of every aspect of our lives.

4.

The day you were born was calm. Your nana, "Dodda," as we call her, offered a silent prayer before I drove your mother to the hospital. All along the way, your mother rehearsed a few lines that she wanted to say to you—words of love and welcome. Any anxiety had now been taken over by the joy surrounding your arrival.

As the clock ticked past 4 pm, my own nerves began to fray. When they rolled your mother into the operating theatre, my heart raced. My hands shook as I waited. I knew you were about to step into this world at any moment, and the gravity of that moment nearly overwhelmed me.

5.

I remembered how your mother would touch her belly and speak to you during her pregnancy. She hoped that you would move, and when you did, she would rejoice in the miracle we had created. The mere thought of you, Isha, growing within your mother's womb was mesmerizing. My greatest joy in life was seeing the miracle I had always known: Isha was finally born.

Your mother went through months of pain and despair, but she held on to her faith. With her resilience, God in the heavens blessed both of us with a bundle of joy. Her body wasn't ready to conceive a baby, but she was—and nothing would stop her from bringing you, Isha, into this world. She gave up so many things she cherished. She often held a glass of wine at social gatherings without taking a sip, and she crossed out blue cheese, sugar, and bread from her list. She cherished every minute of having you inside her, alive and kicking.

Though she might complain about those sacrifices and the cravings she had to control, trust me, she'd do it all over again if it had anything to do with you.

There were two lines she would repeatedly sing and hum: "Isha baby, Isha baby. Come play with me, come play with me." She sang them over and over for you, Isha, believing you could hear her. Your mother knew you were listening and hoped you would move inside her belly. Countless nights passed with her singing herself to sleep, knowing that you were drifting off along with her lullaby.

6.

In the operating room, I was holding your mother's hand as three doctors operated on her. The soft strains of Michael Jackson played faintly in the background, contrasting with the intense focus and the murmur of the doctors in the room. Then, we heard your first cry.

They placed you in my arms, and you held onto me, your tiny fingers wrapping around mine with surprising strength as I cut your umbilical cord. That tiny grasp told me everything I needed to know, you were here, and we belonged together.

You were born with dark hair and eyes wide open. Your mother, despite all her rehearsals, found herself speechless at that moment. When she first held you, tears glistened in her eyes, and at my prompting, all she could manage was a soft, reverent 'Welcome.' That single word, filled with all the love and joy in her heart, was her first to you.

I was overjoyed to see you curled up in a robe, frowning and fidgeting. You held on to my finger and didn't let go.

For the only time in my life, I knew that I had nowhere else to be but with you. You had arrived, and that was enough for my soul.

7.

You were barely over four pounds at the time of your birth, and the doctors rushed you to nursing support. I struggled with an intense wave of emotions and thoughts. I stayed with you, saying my prayers to any God that would respond.

"Protect her, God." I prayed.

And at a lonely point that night, you smiled in your sleep. That was enough for my soul.

8.

I had you up in the room where your mother was recovering. I brought you down from the nursery to spend some time with us. As I held you in my hands, you opened your tiny eyes and touched my face. It was as if you were telling me, 'I'm here now.' In that moment, everything felt complete. I played Kenny Rogers' song 'The Lady,' and these lines felt as if they were written for you: 'Lady, for so many years I thought I'd never find you / You have come into my life and made me whole.' I even have a video of you, less than 12 hours old, touching my face to the sound of that song.

9.

Those days in the nursery are etched in my memory forever. Five times a day, including twice during the quiet hours of the night, I visited you. Those visits became a sacred ritual—changing your diapers, wiping your tiny body, preparing your feed. You had so little strength, barely able to drink 10ml, but I was there, encouraging every sip.

The midwives and nurses would scold me for not doing the swaddle properly, but I was determined to learn, to be there for you every step of the way. Those sleepless nights, the constant worry, the joy of every small progress—it was all worth it. You had arrived, and I was okay, more than okay, was grateful for all of it. I was exactly where I needed to be.

10.

One night, with you still in the nursery, panic struck. I couldn't see your chest move. I didn't know if you were breathing. My heart stopped.

"Isha," I whispered, my voice trembling and barely audible.

No response.

"Isha," I said again, my lips quivering as I held back tears.

I watched, desperate for any sign of life. The steady rhythm of your heartbeat and breathing that I had come to know so well seemed absent. Even in your sleep, you always held onto my finger with all the strength your little hand could muster. But now, there was nothing.

"My baby, Isha," I said, louder this time, panic rising in my throat.

And then you opened your eyes and looked at me. And in that gaze, I found everything: relief, love, connection. Tears streamed down my face as I realized how fragile and precious you were—and how deeply I loved you.

I sang you the lullaby that I had created for you.

〜 〜 〜

You are my darling,
You are my heartbeat,
You are my sunshine,
You are my Am'mā,
You are my everything,
Because you are my Isha.

〜 〜 〜

11.

The day we brought you home, I drove as if the world had slowed down just for you. My hands clenched the wheel, my senses razor-sharp. I carried the most precious cargo of my life, every bump in the road a warning, every turn a prayer. The soft sunlight touched your skin for the very first time, creating a gentle glow that seemed to highlight your perfection. The air outside was a bit chill, but you were peaceful, your tiny face relaxed in contentment. I kept looking back to make sure you were okay, my heart swelling with a mixture of love and protectiveness I had never experienced before. I understood what your grandfather must have felt for me, and I was overwhelmed by the continuity of love across generations. For the first time in my life, I felt complete.

When we reached home, we placed your bassinet on the coffee table, and Milo, our faithful companion, came to investigate. He didn't know who you were, this tiny bundle that suddenly appeared in his home, but somehow, he understood. He sniffed gently, his tail wagging slowly as if to say, "Welcome home, little one. You're part of our family now." It was a beautiful moment of acceptance as our family expanded to include you.

12.

You are a part of a rich heritage and family narrative. As you grow, I hope you'll embrace this legacy while forging your own path. My wish is for you to honor your identity and find strength in your roots as you write your own unique story.

I felt immensely grateful to you for choosing us as your family. Your presence in our lives has filled us with a gratitude we didn't know before. I firmly believe that people choose their families. You chose us. All the lucky stars in the heavens must have aligned, and all the good omens must have bestowed their generosity on me when you chose to step into our lives.

It felt as though I was given the status of a god or someone even superior. I often wonder what luck or cycle of karma had worked in my favor that brought you to me. There could be no joy greater than holding you in my arms. I can never thank you enough for making me a father.

⟨∿⟩ ⟨∿⟩ ⟨∿⟩

Angel's gift, here at last, my daughter, knowing my name
Life's wait over; she's in my arms
Her cry, her smile, her tiny hand
Holding my finger, they say she's mine
Grateful doesn't cover it
She chose me, can you believe it?
What more could I want? At this moment, it's everything.

⟨∿⟩ ⟨∿⟩ ⟨∿⟩

66

As a kid myself, I was carefree and wanted everything in the world, not knowing that the treasure of having a daughter is far greater than all the treasures of the world.

Isha, my darling, you have changed my world in ways I never thought possible. You are my greatest joy and my brightest hope. As you grow, chase wonder. Embrace every challenge. Stay true to yourself, because you are a miracle—one we never stopped believing in. And remember, you are loved beyond measure—now and forever.

Some moments change you forever. Some people enter your life and shift everything you thought you knew. One day, Isha, love will come to you in a way you never expected. When it does, will you choose it—or will it have already chosen you?

I love you more than words can ever express.

Your loving Appā

My dear Isha,
some nights, when the darkness in your dreams would wake you,
you,
you would cry, not knowing what your mind had conjured in your sleep,
your sleep,
and run straight into my room with your hands held out,
knowing well,
a hug will comfort you, a chest awaits to put you back to sleep.
In sleep, you would nestle under my arms and my belly,
resting your head on me and find sleep again to the beating of
my heart and the rhyme of my warm breath,
and as I stay awake, still, watching over you,
as you drifted back into your dreams,
dreams of Gruffalo in our garden playing with your toys,
Of flying dragons, of having tea with Taco,
Of Peppa pig going to school and of things only you can
imagine.
I would softly sing your mother's sleep song with some of my
own words,
"Isha baby, Isha baby, go to sleep, go to sleep,
Appā is here; there is nothing to fear,
Go to sleep; I will always be here".
Only you can dream of things only you can imagine,
your dreams are yours.
Don't let anyone tell you there is no magic in dreaming.
Your mother kept the dream of you going despite knowing her
egg count may be up,
You happened because of her not letting the magic in her dream
fade.
Keep your dreams to yourself. Don't let it fade.
Dream magic. You are that magic.

The Brother You've Yet to Meet

Isha, you have a brother. It's not a secret, nor is it something I have ever tried to hide. Those who need to know are aware. I left my first marriage before he was born. I don't want to speak much about his mother or the details of the relationship—when there's nothing positive to say, it's better left unsaid. I choose not to dwell on certain aspects of that relationship, as there are always two sides to every story, and I prefer to omit my side for fairness to his mother. Silence, in this case, becomes a choice of respect. It's about focusing on what truly matters and what can be learned. She has been a good mother to your brother, and that's enough for me.

I still find it hard to write, as some events from that time take me back to moments of hopelessness I'd rather forget. Revisiting these memories is challenging, but I believe that by sharing them, you both may find strength and understanding in your own journey and trust that there is always a better path ahead if you remain true to who you are.

2.

Life has a way of placing us into circumstances we never anticipated. It tests our resolve, challenges our beliefs, and sometimes forces us to make decisions that stay with us long after. Such was the case with my first marriage.

I entered that union with hope and good intentions, though in hindsight, perhaps I was driven by a misplaced sense of pity—she had been divorced—or maybe I was searching for a sense of belonging, for a family I could call my own. Whatever the reason, I ignored the warnings of those who cautioned me about the challenges we might face, convinced that love, effort, and patience would overcome any obstacle.

I was wrong. Over time, what started as hope turned into something unrecognizable. Love was replaced by control. Fear took root where trust should have been. Doubts grew until they overshadowed everything—alienating my family, dictating the terms of our life together.

It was during this tumultuous time that I learned a hard truth: sometimes, the bravest thing we can do is walk away. I realized that staying in a situation that diminishes your spirit and stifles your growth is not a sacrifice—it's a surrender.

3.

The decision to leave wasn't an easy choice, especially knowing that a child—your half-brother—was on the way. It's a choice that still weighs heavily on me. I walked away from an unborn child, and that's something I've grappled with for years. It was one of the hardest decisions I've ever made, and it shaped my understanding of love, responsibility, and the courage it takes to start over.

But life is about more than the choices we make—it's about how we live with the consequences of those choices afterward. Even though I couldn't stay in that marriage, I never stopped caring for your brother. I've done my best to provide for him and honor my duty as a father through hardship, even from afar.

Still, it's a burden I carry. Walking away from your brother before he was born wasn't just a choice—it was a consequence of choices I had made long before.

4.

This experience taught me that love and relationships cannot thrive under imposed terms and conditions. When it does, it stops being loved and becomes something else—a transaction, a negotiation that costs you your freedom and your authenticity.

Looking back, I realize that life was teaching me lessons I needed to learn. I wasn't ready then; I had to lose some rough edges before I could be prepared for the love and family I have now. These experiences, painful as they were, led me to where I am today—to your mother and to you.

I share this with you not to burden you with my past but to impart a crucial lesson: some connections are better lost if they become too hard to maintain. Some endings, as painful as they may be, can lead to beautiful beginnings. Had I not made that difficult choice, you wouldn't be here, and I can't imagine a world without you in it.

5.

I am sharing this with you as life will present you with many crossroads. Some choices will be clear; others will be heart-wrenchingly difficult. In those moments, I want you to know that it's okay to choose yourself—to walk away from situations that diminish you. But also understand that every choice comes with responsibility. Whatever you decide, face the consequences with dignity and honor your commitments.

You are the product of many loves, many choices, and, yes, some regrets. But you are also the promise of a future where lessons learned can create something beautiful. As you forge your own path, know that I'll always be here to support you through whatever comes your way.

6.

I sincerely hope that as your brother grows up, he develops a broader perspective on life and cultivates an abundant mindset. Life has so much to offer when approached with openness and positivity. I wish for him to choose a path that leads to growth and fulfillment, just as I wish the same for you.

I worry about the future. I want you to understand that true security comes from self-reliance. I want both of you to strive for independence, to take pride in your own efforts. The environment your brother is growing up in encourages reliance on assistance in ways that don't sit right with me. I don't want that path for either of you. Such a life can make you hollow inside, often leading to dishonesty and a loss of self-respect. It's a dishonorable way to live, relying on the system rather than on your own abilities and efforts.

I hope your brother doesn't adopt a mindset that glorifies or depends on assistance. Instead, I wish for both of you to strive for self-reliance, to find purpose in your work, and to take pride in supporting yourselves. This doesn't mean you should never seek help when truly needed, but it does mean valuing your independence and the dignity that comes from earning your own way in life.

7.

Isha, I hope that one day, you and your brother will meet—not out of obligation, but out of curiosity, connection, and choice. Circumstances have kept you apart, but you share a bond through me. Maybe one day, that will mean something. Your paths may be different, but there's potential for understanding, support, and even friendship between you.

Family is rarely simple. Sometimes, it does not fit the shape we expect. But when the time comes, I hope you will choose what family means to you—not by obligation, but by heart.

I dream of a future where you both might share stories, learn from each other's experiences, and perhaps find common ground in the challenges and joys of life. Family connections can be complex, but they can also be a source of unexpected strength and enrichment.

Whether and how you choose to pursue this relationship will be your decision, but I want you to know that I would be happy to see a positive connection between you two, should you both desire it.

Life is shaped by the choices we make and the mindset we carry. Never let circumstances define your limits or shrink your dreams. The strength to build the life you want is already within you.

Yours always, Appā

Every Family Has Secrets

Dear Isha,

Every family has secrets; we all have them. Some secrets come out over time, while others stay hidden forever. But sometimes, life creates opportunities to open small windows to uncover these secrets—a moment that changes everything and also offers a chance to change. I had such an experience one rainy afternoon that forever altered how I saw our family.

It had been raining for a week during that monsoon season. On that afternoon, as I walked home from school, strong winds blew through the streets. This usually meant there were fallen mangoes waiting to be found. The air was thick with the smell of wet earth and ripe fruit, a strong scent that stuck to everything. I took the longer way home, enjoying the sight of mango trees with their branches full of heavy fruit. The wind shook the trees, and ripe mangoes fell to the wet ground. Soaked but happy, I picked up the fallen fruits, their sweet smell mixing with the earthy scent of the rain-soaked ground.

Recently, your grandfather had been in an accident. A car had struck him from behind, and he was lucky to be alive. His spine was badly injured, leaving him bedridden for months. We lived in the staff quarters just behind the hotel where he worked, in a small, close-knit community where everyone knew everyone else's business. Usually, we didn't have many visitors, but lately, during his recovery, his coworkers often came by to check on him and our house had become a hub.

As I neared our house that day, I saw two boys around my age standing outside. I didn't recognize them. One of them was talking with someone inside while the other stood quietly. Their presence felt strange, out of place in the familiar surroundings of my daily life.

I greeted them casually, mentioning that your grandfather couldn't return to work for another month. One of the boys responded, "I know; Dad was just telling us."

The word **"Dad"** hit me hard. I froze. The rain soaking through my clothes suddenly didn't matter.

I knew people sometimes called my father "Daddy" at work, but there was something different here, there was a familiarity in his voice that unsettled me.

The door was partly open, and inside, I could see my father lying in bed, his head propped up. His eyes were wet, and he gave me a look that felt like it carried more than I could understand at that age. He managed a smile, but it wasn't one I recognised.

Before they left, one of the boys, the shorter one with a faint mustache placed a hand on my shoulder, his tone serious in a way that caught me off guard.

"Can I talk to you for a minute?" he asked.

He handed me a piece of paper with a phone number scribbled on it, "It's our house phone number," he said. "Call us if something like this happens again. He is our dad, too."

The words hit like a punch.

Then he added, "We, as kids, shouldn't have to pay for our parents' mistakes. We are brothers."

I stood frozen. The number in my hand wasn't just a string of digits—it was a door into a part of my father's life that had been hidden from me. It was a connection I hadn't known existed, one that would tie us together in ways I didn't yet understand.

2.

When I stepped into the house, I was met with an unusual silence, the air thick with tension that overshadowed even the familiar scents of home. Your grandmother moved through the kitchen like a ghost, her stiff posture saying a lot. Seeing my father's teary eyes and my mother's rigid posture, I felt my world shift and crumble. My safe family haven shattered into something unfamiliar that I no longer recognized. I didn't know what had happened.

Your grandfather lay in bed, his eyes brimming with a mix of shame, regret, and fear. The strong, dependable man I had always known seemed to have disappeared, replaced by someone who appeared smaller, more diminished—not just from his physical injuries but from the weight of the truth he could no longer hide.

In that moment, Isha, my safe family haven, transformed into something unfamiliar and frightening: a place of unanswered questions. The weight of this new knowledge pressed down on me, affecting every interaction. Family meals, once a time for relaxed conversation, now became silent and strained.

It wasn't long before forgotten memories of conversations came back to me with startling clarity. I remembered your grandmother previously saying many times, which I had once tuned out, now echoed: "Your father abandoned us." A statement I'd brushed off at the time now resonated deeply, cutting into the safe illusions I'd held about our family.

Navigating this new reality was challenging. I found myself avoiding your grandfather's room, overwhelmed by the surge of emotions. Our small house offered no escape, the confined spaces only amplifying the silence among us. Complicating matters, this secret remained unknown to my sisters. I chose not to tell them, but I think they knew—their years of living through his absence had likely revealed more than words ever could.

Over time, life at home slowly found its way back to some normalcy. The initial shock and tension gradually eased into a routine, though an undercurrent of unspoken truths lingered. Your grandmother's resilience was pivotal during this transition. She kept up the rhythm of our daily lives—ensuring meals were prepared, homework was completed, and managing the household—with a quiet determination that earned my deep admiration. Your grandfather also strived to rebuild trust, taking a more active role in our lives once he recovered. Family dinners regained their usual chatter, and laughter once again filled our home. Yet, beneath this surface of normalcy, I sensed a profound change. Our family had been tested, and while we had weathered the storm, we were undeniably changed by the experience.

Your grandmother's decision to hold our family together, despite the deep pain and betrayal, was a testament to her incredible strength. This choice, profound in its implications, would shape our lives in ways we could not yet foresee. I watched her care for your grandfather-giving him his medicines, tending to his needs, and even feeding him at times—while also supporting the rest of us with unwavering grace. Yet, in brief moments, I could see the raw resentment in her eyes.

I could understand her anger, resentment, or even not being willing to forgive fully. I began to see forgiveness differently—not as something offered lightly, but as a choice that demanded strength. It wasn't an effortless gift but something fought for. It was a struggle, something you had to fight for. It took strength and resilience, a willingness to rebuild trust shattered by betrayal. A choice made over and over again, even when trust lay in pieces.

It wasn't until my university days that I began to truly grasp the complexity of what had occurred. Time and distance had given me room to reflect, but the questions I carried remained sharp, unanswered. Immersed in my studies and introspection, my thoughts often returned to that rainy afternoon and everything that followed. My notebooks became cluttered with thoughts, scattered and messy, as I tried to make sense of everything. Each page was a step in understanding the subtleties of family dynamics, love, forgiveness, and personal identity.

One evening, years after that fateful day, when the house was quiet and my father was asleep, I found my mother in the kitchen. The questions that had been burning inside me for so long finally spilled out.

"Why, Amma?" I asked, my voice shaking with emotion. "Why did you take Appā back?"

She looked at me, slightly taken aback by the question, and with all the betrayal flashing before her, her emotions laid bare; her eyes met mine, heavy with tiredness, still holding on to the anger she thought she'd buried, and despite the years a sadness filled her. She knew what I was asking exactly.

"For my children, for us," she said softly, her voice tinged with both love and bitterness, "love isn't just about the happiness or good times. It's about staying with someone even when they've caused you pain, particularly when they've hurt you. Your father made a terrible mistake—one I've been grappling with since before you were born. But he's still your father, still my husband. I stayed because our family was worth fighting for, even when I wasn't sure I'd win".

Her words left me speechless. I was torn between admiration for her resilience and disbelief at the bitterness she carried. In that moment, I glimpsed the enormity of her love—not just for my father, our family, and me. I realized her love was layered—full of pain but also rooted in a quiet, unshakable strength. It was a love that transcended betrayal and chose to stay, even though the pain never left.

Isha, this experience shaped my understanding of love and family. It taught me that people are not simply good or bad, right or wrong. We are all capable of both profound love and deep hurt. I learned that love isn't always straightforward or pure; it can be messy, painful, and complex. But this also revealed to me the power of forgiveness and the formidable strength required to keep a family together.

I have been through betrayals and life circumstances that didn't feel fair, and I find it hard to forgive and let go. Forgiveness isn't easy—it's a struggle. Be kind to yourself if it feels hard; it's not something anyone masters overnight. As you navigate your own relationships, remember this story. Value authenticity and seek connections that can stand the test of time.

Forgiveness isn't weakness—it's strength.

Life will test your heart. Let it teach you to love deeper, not harden you.

We are all flawed. We hurt. We fail. And yet, we are still worthy of love, still deserving of forgiveness.

Hold onto love, Isha. It is the one thing that will always bring you home. It's the one thing that keeps us whole.

Always, Appā

The Strength in Forgiveness

Isha, let me tell you about my early life with my parents.

My parents never owned a toothbrush until very late in their lives. Not because they couldn't afford it but because they didn't see it as a necessity. Their needs always came second. We, their children, came first.

My mother was always the last one to eat. Not just my mother, but your Nana, 'Dodda' as you call her, would never eat first. She would wait for others to serve themselves before she served herself. And if there was any leftover rice from the previous night, she would never place it on the table; she would serve herself that rice. Your maternal grandfather, your 'Thatha,' likewise, would never take the first roti at the dining table. He would always reach for the roti at the bottom, wanting others to have the warm ones on top.

These small, everyday gestures—unnoticed—are what stay with me now. They weren't or aren't grand or loud, but they carry the depth of their devotion to their family.

2.

We didn't have a big house. It was a 200-square-feet, one-bedroom unit at most. My sisters slept in the bedroom, and I slept in the living room with my parents. The unit was small enough that no conversation could be private, and there was nothing in the house that wasn't shared. But back then, we didn't know any better, and I believe it is because of that we kids were content. "Content" is a broad word, I won't say that we were content; we were happy. We had each other, and somehow, that was enough.

We didn't go on holiday except to my Nan's house in Mangadu. We didn't have many relatives coming over; it was nearly impossible to accommodate them when they did. And we didn't have a TV for most of my childhood. And when we did, there wasn't much on TV to watch. Back then, there was only one state-run TV channel with a few hours of programming each day based on a socialistic narrative set by the federal government of the day. Our exposure to the outside world was very limited, be it through lived experiences or television. But that didn't matter much to us and held little significance. The world beyond our home seemed far, like a story that didn't belong to us. Because of this, our family's—or at least my—perspective on grander things and aspirations for bigger dreams didn't come up until late in my life when I started reading English literature. Despite the limited exposure, there were certain moments that shifted my outlook and my view on life.

I remember once coming back home late after a long day outside, loitering or playing cricket. I am not sure why I was out so late that day—I don't really recall—but it was late enough that my sisters had already eaten. I was hungry. It was one of those hungers where you can sense it moving inside; you don't feel the pain, but you can tell your stomach is empty.

When I walked in, my mother was waiting for me. She didn't scold me or ask why I was late. I told her I was very hungry and tired. As I mentioned before, our house wasn't big, so I could hear her in the kitchen preparing a plate for me. I heard her scraping the bottom of the vessel but thought nothing of it. She handed me the plate and walked away. I asked her to sit and eat with me, knowing she was always the last one to eat, but she brushed it off, saying she would eat a bit later.

It didn't occur to me then what had happened. But something tugged at me. I went to the kitchen under the pretense of getting water and saw the empty pot. There was nothing left. She had scraped together what was left at the bottom for me.

I was almost in tears at what she was willing to do for me. I didn't say anything. I ate a few morsels and told her I was full. I put the plate back in the kitchen with some food still on it.

A little later, she sat down to finish that plate, sitting alone on the floor in the kitchen in the narrow space between the pantry and the fridge under a dim 40w bulb, lost in her thoughts.

I sat beside her. I didn't know what to say. Finally, I asked her, apologetic and full of guilt, "Why didn't you tell me there was no food left for you, Amma?"

She just smiled, that soft, knowing smile of hers. "You are my son," she said as if those words explained everything. She then took a handful of rice from her plate and fed it to me. That was enough for me. Her simple words, "You are my son," carried a depth I couldn't fully grasp then—the pain and sacrifices she was willing to bear for us.

My perspective on parents and food changed that night. Something in me shifted. The weight of her sacrifice, the depth of her love, hit me in a way I hadn't felt before. For the first time, I saw my mother not just as a parent, as my Amma, but as a person, a woman with her own hopes, dreams, struggles, and, above all, her own hunger. And she had given all of that up for us, her children. I couldn't sleep that night. Questions that had probably always been there, just beneath the surface, began to take shape. They had been unspoken, dismissed but now they demanded attention. Why had my mother, despite her own hunger, given me that last bowl of rice? Why didn't my parents use a toothbrush?

Why did my mother always eat late and alone? Why did they pay for our education despite their hardships? These "whys" and "whats" seemed to surround me, echoing in every corner of my thoughts.

Behind these questions was a single, undeniable truth: their lives were defined by selflessness—an unwavering dedication to family above all. Looking back, I can see that their belief in our future was what made them let go of their present.

Their sacrifices, both big and small, were threads woven into the fabric of our family. Each act of selflessness, each moment of putting their children's needs ahead of their own, created a foundation of love and resilience that supported our lives.

3.

This foundation was tested time and time again, but never more than when we faced the profound loss of your grandfather, my father. His passing was a defining moment for our family, bringing to the surface the complex emotions and experiences that had shaped my parents' relationship over the years.

My father's death marked the end of an era—a moment that should have been filled with overwhelming grief, a wife bidding farewell to her lifelong partner. But for my mother, the grief was complex and layered, shaped by decades of shared history, love, disappointment, and reconciliation.

She stood by his side, a woman caught between mourning the loss of the man she once loved—the father of her children—and grappling with the pain of his betrayals.

My mother's eyes, usually so full of life, were now shadowed with deep sorrow. She had spent a lifetime with this man, raising children, building a home, and enduring hardships. Yet, as she stood there, she couldn't ignore the pain of the years he had been absent—the time he spent with another woman, leaving her to fend for herself and our family.

She grieved in her own way. There was no loud wailing or cries, as is common in South Indian traditions. Instead, she stood stoic and resolute, her face a mix of pain and resolve. Her grief carried the weight of broken trust and the strength she had taken to survive and care for her family alone.

As she held his hand, memories rushed back. She remembered the young, passionate man she married, full of dreams and ambitions. He had been her partner, her confidant, and her greatest source of joy—if only for a time.

She remembered the early days of their marriage, filled with love, laughter, and shared dreams. Married life was all smiles and bliss. My Nana lived next door to her daughter's in-laws, and it was all convenient, seeming like part of a divine plan. But the realities of building a life together soon set in. My father had to return to Madras for work, leaving his young bride behind. The distance was a test of their love, but it was one they were determined to pass.

My father made frequent fortnight visits, using every excuse he could to see my mother. He brought her small tokens of his affection—perfumes to remind her of his presence, hair oil to keep her locks shining, talcum powders to soothe her skin, and colorful bangles to adorn her wrists. These gifts though, weren't extravagant, were more than just objects; they were thoughtful and tangible reminders that she was in his mind.

As time went on, their love continued to grow, and new opportunities arose. Their love story took on a different shade when my father found a government job in New Delhi, a city he had never visited before. It was good money, and he was working for the government. It offered him the assurance that he could now promise his young bride a bigger life, a life that wasn't just about surviving but living comfortably.

This decision was met with a lot of apprehension from my Nana, as she wasn't happy about her daughter going far away to a land where they spoke a different language and had a different lifestyle. She wasn't sure how her daughter would manage it all on her own. And rightly so, as my mother had never ventured far from the village.

Life in New Delhi was everything they had spoken about, full of firsts. Together, alone for the first time, it felt like they were truly a couple. It was a much simpler time. Independent India was just a few years old, there was optimism everywhere, and the young couple had enough money to even go on holiday.

But their trips, meant to be romantic getaways, often fell short of expectations. A visit to the Taj Mahal left them underwhelmed, but the young couple made the most of it by spending time in Agra's night markets, shopping, and enjoying local street food. A winter trip to Shimla, with a young son in tow, proved to be more challenging than enchanting. These experiences, though disappointing in the moment, would later become cherished memories, stories to be retold with a mix of laughter and nostalgia.

The real challenges, however, were yet to come. The allure of their new life in Delhi began to fade, and my mother found herself longing for the familiarity of home. The weather, the food, the language—everything felt foreign to her. With my father busy with work and his still active social life, the burden of parenthood fell heavily on her shoulders. She struggled, and for the first time in their married life, tension flared in a big way. Eventually, my mother returned home and began living with her mother.

4.

Life carried on with its challenges and hardships. For years, my parents lived apart—my father worked first out of Delhi and later in Bangalore. Beneath the surface, cracks were forming but were manageable. And then came the betrayal– a moment that redefined their marriage.

The news came unexpectedly through a slip of the tongue. Someone visiting from Bangalore let it slip that my father had been living with another woman. My mother's world crumbled in an instant. Each word was a dagger to her heart. She sank to the floor, her body shaking with sobs, as the life she had built with him shattered before her eyes. The trust she had placed in him, the years they had spent building a life together—it felt like a lie. The pain was visceral, a physical ache that consumed her every waking moment.

Even in her despair, she found solace in the unwavering love she had for her children and clung to that. By now, she had four children—the eldest born during her time in Delhi, and the other three in Mangadu. She drew strength from their need for her, knowing she was their anchor in the storm.

5.

When my father finally returned for good, there was no grand apology, no dramatic gestures of remorse. Eventually, he brought his family to Bangalore, securing a staff quarters behind the hotel where he worked. It marked the beginning of a new chapter for our family. He simply slipped back into the role of husband and father as if nothing had changed. But everything had. The trust that had once held my parents together was gone, and rebuilding would take years. But I doubt it ever truly happened at all.

Forgiveness was not easy. If it came at all, it was not immediate. My mother bore the pain quietly, letting it seep into her silence. She grappled with the anger, the sense of betrayal, and the fear of an uncertain future. There were moments when she wanted to give up, to let the bitterness consume her. She had to find her way through it, not for herself, but for us. But in the end, she chose the harder path—the path of forgiveness. And this came from a place of strength. Her love for us was her strength, and that strength was what eventually helped her rebuild her life.

My mother's resilience in the face of betrayal and hardship stands as a powerful testament to the strength of the human spirit. Her ability to forgive my father and rebuild their relationship—not just for herself but for the well-being of her children—shows the transformative power of empathy and understanding. Even in the darkest of times, her story is a reminder that healing and reconciliation are always possible.

Life carried on, though it was never quite the same. My father carried a look of quiet defeat, a shadow of the man he once was. My mother, despite her resilience, always seemed to hold onto a trace of anger, a reminder of the betrayal she had endured. And yet, somehow, they made it work.

Over time, they rebuilt—not to what they once were, but to something new. A bond, not untouched, but tested and worn. The process was slow, trust rebuilt in small, careful steps. They had to learn each other again, to unlearn the past, to find a way forward. It was a dance of two steps forward and one step back, but they kept moving.

I am in awe of how they managed it—how they stayed together through it all, determined to get us, their children, to a place of safety and stability. Their love may not have been perfect, but it was powerful in its persistence. Even in the darkest of times, they showed that healing and reconciliation, though imperfect, are possible when there is a shared purpose and unwavering commitment.

6.

The income that was once considered sufficient was hardly enough to survive. With four children still in primary school and only one income to depend on, life was challenging. Yet, despite these difficulties, my parents were united by a common purpose: the well-being of their children. Their love for us was the glue that held them together, even when the world around them seemed to be falling apart. They put aside their personal grievances to ensure that we had a stable and loving home.

In the early days of his career, my father used to work the afternoon shifts, often finishing late, around 11 at night. When he got home, he would take me, already asleep, out of bed, place me on his lap, and talk to my mother well into the night. It was their ritual. My mother would sit beside him, and they would talk.

I remember one night when their voices grew louder, a heated argument breaking the usual rhythm of their conversation. I woke up startled, but my father quickly lowered his voice. As he gently patted me back to sleep, I heard him whisper, "Please forgive me."

I didn't understand what he was apologizing for back then, but I saw my mother crying, her eyes glistening with tears in the dim light. The next morning, I asked him why he had said sorry. He just laughed softly and gave me a hug.

These moments, these raw and honest exchanges, were the building blocks of their reconciliation. They were learning, slowly and painfully, especially for my mother, how to trust him again.

I learned the importance of forgiveness and empathy. I saw firsthand how open communication and a willingness to understand each other's perspectives could heal even the deepest wounds. I am not going to lie or pretend that these lessons have fully shaped my own approach to relationships. I'm far from perfect in practicing empathy or understanding, and I may not be the best person to offer advice on either.

My parents' lives were a testament to the idea that true fulfillment comes from dedicating oneself to a cause greater than personal desires. They sacrificed their personal dreams to ensure we had opportunities they never did. My father, in particular, let go of his passion to provide for the family. He found joy in our achievements, knowing he had given us the tools to succeed.

Their relationship evolved into one of mutual respect and admiration, held together largely for the sake of us children. Despite the challenges and conflicts they faced, their commitment to our upbringing became the foundation that allowed us to thrive beyond what society and the community expected of us or believed we could achieve. We are glad we didn't get sucked into their limiting beliefs.

I once asked my father why they put us through expensive education when that money could be used for necessities. He answered simply: they believed in something bigger for us. They knew that good education was the key to a future they could only dream of, and they were determined to make it possible.

7.

In those final moments by my father's bedside, my mother reflected on a lifetime of memories—the love, the hurt, the betrayal, and the forgiveness that had woven together the complex story of their shared life. With tears streaming down her face, she whispered words of love and gratitude for all they had endured and the family they had built together.

Their story was not one of perfection but perseverance. They had weathered storms that would have broken others, emerging stronger for it. Their love, imperfect as it was, had been the foundation of our family.

As my mother faced the future without her lifelong partner, she knew that his legacy would live on through the family they had nurtured together.

Isha, I hope you see now the depth of love and sacrifice that shaped our family. Your grandparents' journey was not perfect, but it was real—marked by resilience, by forgiveness, by love that endured even when it was tested.

True love is not about perfection. It is about growing together, forgiving deeply, and choosing each other—again and again.

Their story is a part of you, woven into the fabric of who you are. Let it guide you as a source of strength and a reminder that even in the darkest moments, love has the power to light the way home.

One day, you might find yourself at the edge of forgiveness, unsure if you can take that step. When that moment comes, ask yourself: What is worth holding on to, and what is worth setting free?

Oh, and Isha—brush your teeth. My father didn't. By 50, most of them were gone.

Always remember, you come from a family that has known love in all its messiness and still chose to hold on. Carry that forward.

Love, Appā

What Love Becomes

Isha,

I often ask your mother why she married me, and her answer is always the same: she loves me. I always pause at that reply. I pause not because I doubt her feelings, but because love is a word I've never fully understood in the way the world defines it. What we have is something else—years of shared experiences, trust, and an unspoken understanding that binds us together. Maybe that is its own kind of love.

I've rewritten this paragraph countless times, but in the end, I decided to keep it simple and have removed a few lines. While being raw and honest can be admirable, in the complexities of marriage and long-term commitment, it can sometimes lead to more pain.

I know many in our family might be upset by this, but when I ask them to define the emotion they feel for their partner, the answers often sound like borrowed lines—Shakespearean verses, or Keats' poetry or words lifted from a Valentine's Day card. However, many would struggle to explain the intricate layers of love and connection that develop over time. Is their relationship rooted in love, or is it simply a bond built through familiarity and shared existence?

I believe what I have with your mother is a connection.

Love and marriage mean different things to different people. There's a distinction between love and the deep connection that forms over time through shared experiences. Love is something else entirely. It consumes a person, becomes their very reason for being, and drives everything they do. It reshapes who you are. It weaves another person into your very identity, so deeply that their happiness becomes your own.

But connection by association is different. It's the presence of another person in your life growing so significantly that they become indispensable to you, both physically and emotionally.

When I married your mother, some close friends of ours questioned my decision. Some were blunt, while others were more tactful, considering the sensitivity of the topic. My answer to all of them was the same: "She will be there for me and with me, no matter what."

I wasn't someone who planned to marry again. I had closed that chapter the day I walked out of my first marriage. To be honest, I didn't have the resources, I hadn't achieved the career success I wanted by the age of 40, and I wasn't sure how I could support another person with what little I had. I was content with my life as it was. But your mother was determined from the very first day we met—she wanted a long-term commitment and marriage. I told her that I had just walked out of a marriage and wasn't interested in entering another one.

About three months after the Sydney family court finalized my divorce, I was invited to meet your mother's extended family, who were visiting from India. We gathered at Circular Quay for drinks, and the topic of marriage inevitably came up. In a South Indian household, it's very common for parents and family members to openly discuss marriage. That evening, I told your mother that this was not acceptable, as she knew very well how I felt about marriage. There was also a feeling that I was holding her back from a better life and that the best thing I could do was step out of the picture. So, that evening, I shook hands with them, turned my back and I walked away from your mother as far as I could.

A year and a half later, I was at work when I received a message from your mother. She wanted to meet.

We met at a coffee house in Circular Quay at the beginning of summer. She still had that beautiful smile and a radiance about her that I couldn't forget. And just like that, I knew I had never really left her. She confessed that she was willing to move in with me, even without marriage on the table. She was living with her parents and planning to move out. Despite my reservations about marriage, I couldn't deny the connection we shared. Your mother's persistence and willingness to compromise showed me her dedication and adaptability—qualities I've come to deeply respect in her.

A few months later, we bought a house and moved in together. Those early days of living together were filled with hope and shared dreams. We worked well together, setting up our home and planning for the future. Your mother's organizational skills and eye for detail complemented my more laid-back approach, creating a balance that served us well.

Three years after we moved in, I married her. She was pregnant with you two months later. I married her because it meant something to her, and there was also a cultural expectation weighing heavily on having a child born out of wedlock.

Then came the fall. My own missteps, my own blind spots—I lost my money—and some of your mother's too. With that loss came a loss of honor and respect in our household. Like my father before me, I went from being a man content with his life to one stripped of dignity, no longer seen as someone who made mistakes but as a complete failure.

Your mother has been a pillar of strength when I needed it most. She stood by me through my financial wreckage. Even in our darkest financial moments, your mother's resourcefulness shone through. She found ways to stretch our budget and keep our household running, demonstrating a strength and practicality that I truly admired. But this came at a cost. I began to feel that I had no influence over how our marriage functioned. The weight of my failures, the loss of money, the loss of intimacy, and the sense of powerlessness in our relationship created a perfect storm within me. It was around this time that I decided I couldn't stay. It was my time to leave this world.

These thoughts were dark and consuming. The idea of leaving it all behind seemed like the only escape from the pain and emptiness I felt. But even in those moments, a small part of me held on—for you, for the future, for the slim hope that things might change.

I hope that by the time you're reading this, you're old enough to grasp the weight of these feelings and the importance of seeking help when needed. I reached out to a hotline, but almost immediately, I began to regret it. The regret came from the routine of having to speak to a doctor or therapist three or four times a day, repeatedly recounting my emotions, followed by nurse visits every other day and daily calls. I suppose that's how the help works. But it wasn't helping me. The tablets they prescribed gave me headaches and made me nauseous.

Going through this dark period taught me the importance of resilience and the power of perseverance. While the challenges in my marriage persisted, I found ways to rediscover my sense of self-worth beyond the confines of our relationship. I started to write my feelings and thoughts unfiltered. It wasn't easy, and it's an ongoing process, but it's a journey I'm committed to—for myself and for you. These letters are part of that process.

I share this with you not to burden you but to help you understand the complexities of adult relationships and mental health. Life will present you with challenges, some of which may feel overwhelming. In those moments, remember that you're not alone, that help is available, and that even the darkest nights eventually give way to dawn.

What exists between your mother and me may sometimes seem broken, but there is one thing that remains unshakable—a bond united in one purpose, and that is you. Despite our struggles, your mother and I have shared moments of joy and accomplishment, particularly in raising you. Her dedication as a mother, her ability to anticipate your needs, and her unwavering support of your dreams have been invaluable. In you, I see the best of both of us— a testament to the positive aspects of our union.

I'm not here to cast anyone in a negative light but rather to help you understand that relationships, especially marriages, can be incredibly complex. Love, commitment, and family often intertwine in ways that aren't always clear-cut or easy to explain. And I want you to know that when you lose your way, it takes time to get back up. As my father felt in his later years, one's prominence will fade, and the world around will move on.

I want you to know that despite these complexities, the love we both have for you is real and unwavering. You are the beautiful outcome of our union, the purpose that keeps us together.

As you grow and form your own relationships, remember that they rarely fit into perfect, simple narratives. Be honest with yourself and your partner about your feelings and expectations. And above all, make choices that are true to who you are.

Be in love. Fully, fiercely. But if you think marriage is the only way to prove that love, stop. Love doesn't need validation. It needs truth.

Love changes, Isha. It is never just one thing.

But through all its changes, may you always know this: real love is not about proving anything to the world—it is about what feels true to you.

Appā

Part 3: Challenges and Redemption

(resilience, struggle, growth)

Isha, life does not move in straight lines. It will break you, rebuild you, and sometimes leave you standing in the wreckage, wondering what comes next. I have seen failure. I have carried shame. I have made mistakes that felt impossible to recover from. And yet, I am still here.

This section holds the hardest stories I have to tell—the ones shaped by loss, missteps, and the slow climb back. Some of these moments may feel heavy, but I want you to know that struggle does not define you. Growth happens in the spaces between what we hoped for and what life gives us. And redemption? It is never out of reach, even when it feels like it is.

You will face your own challenges, Isha. When that time comes, I hope you remember this: you are not your worst days. You are not your failures. You are everything that comes after them.

From My Dad to Me and Now to You

Isha

There are moments in life that shape us, often in ways we don't fully understand until years later. My relationship with my father was never straightforward. It shifted through phases—holding different meanings at different times. He was the father I loved and admired, then someone I felt embarrassed by, and finally, a man I came to deeply respect and revere.

I want to share some moments with him that changed how I saw him and, in turn, myself. These memories are a window into my own journey of understanding family, identity, and love.

One of my earliest memories happened when I was about eight years old. It was summer, and the rains had failed that year. One afternoon, your grandfather hurriedly took me out of the hotel where he worked and where we lived in the back. A large crowd had gathered near our state's Chief Minister's official residence, Cauvery, which was next to the hotel. The Chief Minister of Tamil Nadu, MGR, as they called him, was coming to meet our state's Chief Minister to discuss the water issue and to request the release of water from the Cauvery River dam.

This wasn't just any water dispute. The Cauvery River, flowing from our state into Tamil Nadu, had been a source of contention for over 100 years. When the rains failed, there often wasn't enough water left for Tamil Nadu after the farmers upstream in our state took their share. This left the river in Tamil Nadu dry, affecting millions of lives and countless acres of crops.

As MGR's car approached, the crowd's excitement became palpable. The air was charged with both anger and hope. The crowd was mostly Tamils, many carrying banners and flags demanding the immediate release of water and the opening of the dams. There was also a section of people who were simply there to see the man himself, who was also a cinema star. My father, who never took an interest in politics, was there just to see him and had brought me along to show me the man from his homeland.

I also noticed supporters of the Tamil cause in Sri Lanka holding placards demanding an end to cultural genocide. The place was heavily secured, with police on both sides of the road, and a cacophony of slogans in Tamil and broken Kannada filled the air. I was too young to grasp the significance of the visit, but I was very curious to see the man who had drawn so much attention. My father, who knew some of the police guarding the area, managed to get us to the front of the crowd, close to the gates.

Then, after dozens of cars passed, I saw him—MGR, in his trademark white cap and dark glasses, and as his car passed, he waved. Being the only child at the front, I caught his eye, and he waved directly at me. It didn't mean much to me then, but my father was visibly excited about this moment and spoke about it for weeks afterward.

The next day, the dams were opened. While the decision brought relief to the farmers in Tamil Nadu, it sparked outrage in our state. Tensions escalated everywhere—even in my small school.

2.

This decision had unexpected consequences for me at school. I attended a newly opened school and was part of its first class—just eight students who moved through the grades together. We were a close-knit group, and these seven classmates were my whole world.

Our class teacher was passionate about local causes. She viewed people like my father, migrants from Tamil Nadu, as taking good jobs from locals. With the water release, she felt her people were being deprived of what was rightfully theirs. Though she didn't name me, her statement in the class that "Tamils need to go back" left no doubt about who she meant.

The message was clear. My classmates heard it. And they obeyed. The next day, no one spoke to me. No one played with me. Just like that, I was alone. Suddenly, I found myself isolated from the only social circle I'd ever known. The ostracism lasted for weeks, and it was deeply hurtful. These weren't just classmates; they were my closest friends, the only world I knew. I was suddenly an outsider.

When the school eventually apologized to your grandfather, I expected him to stand up for me. Your grandfather's reaction puzzled and angered me. He apologized instead, assuming I had done something wrong. When I tried to explain, he told me to "get along." His response hurt more than the teacher's words. I felt unprotected and misunderstood.

But the damage was done. I felt betrayed, not just by my teacher, but by the friends I thought I could trust. And I was also angry at my father, who had refused to believe me until then. I hated him for it.

Looking back, I see it differently. He wasn't dismissing my pain— he was teaching me the cost of survival. In his world, standing out was dangerous. Blending in was safer.

At the time, I only felt anger. Now, I see the weight he carried.

3.

This anger simmered, shaping my young mind in ways I couldn't fully comprehend at the time. I began to see my Tamil identity as a burden, something to hide rather than embrace. In the privacy of my thoughts, I started crafting a new version of myself, one that excluded the parts of me linked to Tamil culture.

At home, Tamil was the language of love and comfort—the tongue in which your grandmother sang lullabies, your grandfather told stories, and we, as a family, spoke. But outside, it became a secret language, one I was reluctant to use. I found myself hesitating to speak Tamil in public, fearing it would mark me as an outsider.

I knew so little of Tamil culture beyond what I'd absorbed at home. Our television showed no Tamil programs, we never went to the cinema to watch Tamil movies, and the books in my school library rarely mentioned Tamil history or traditions. The richness of my heritage—its music, ancient literature, and vibrant festivals— remained a mystery to me, a world I could sense but not fully access.

We visited Mangadu in Tamil Nadu every year, providing some connection to my roots. But these visits were brief, not long enough to fully immerse me in the culture. The scarcity of relatives visiting us further distanced me from our traditions. It was as though I was looking through a window into a world that was supposed to be mine, yet it felt foreign.

I began to notice this disconnect even in how I viewed your grandfather. His stories of growing up in Tamil Nadu, the traditions he tried to maintain, and the foods he lovingly prepared all began to feel foreign to me. Our annual trips offered fleeting moments of connection, but they weren't enough to bridge the growing gap between his world and mine. His life experiences felt like echoes from a distant land I no longer recognized as my own.

I felt lost between two worlds, belonging to neither. At school, I was the Tamil boy, defined by my name and my family's background. At home, I was growing increasingly estranged from the culture that had shaped your grandfather's life. This dual existence was exhausting, leaving me feeling like a perpetual outsider, never quite fitting in anywhere.

As I grew, this complex relationship with my identity and your grandfather continued to shape me. It influenced the friends I chose, the interests I pursued, and even the dreams I dared to dream. I found myself gravitating towards anything that seemed 'local,' desperately trying to prove that I belonged while simultaneously feeling a deep, unspoken guilt for distancing myself from my roots.

Your grandfather, with his strong accent unique to Tamil speakers and his traditional ways, became a constant reminder of everything I was trying to leave behind. His pride in his heritage, which should have been a source of strength for me, instead became a point of conflict. I couldn't understand why he held so tightly to a culture that seemed to bring nothing but hardship and discrimination.

4.

It took years for me to appreciate the depth of your grandfather's connection to his culture. What I didn't realize then was the stark difference between our lives at the same age. When I was 13, sheltered and comfortable at home, your grandfather was already on the streets, working various jobs at an eatery. He had left his parents' home, building his life from nothing. He managed to survive in circumstances I can scarcely imagine. For years, I had failed to recognize, appreciate, and honor that incredible journey.

Once, while still in primary school, I was asked about my future aspirations. Without hesitation, I said I wanted to be a chef like my father. While other children dreamed of becoming doctors or scientists, my vision was shaped by what I knew best—the world of your grandfather.

What I didn't understand then was how deeply my early life was entwined with your grandfather's profession. From just a few months old, he had been my primary caretaker. My mother, when she had chores and when my sisters were too much to manage, would drop me off at his workplace, just minutes from our home, and I'd spend hours in the hotel kitchen while he cooked. The hotel kitchen became my daycare center. The bustle, sounds, and aromas became the comforting backdrop of my childhood; I often preferred it over staying at home with my sisters. This routine continued until the hotel tightened its occupational safety rules, and your grandfather's manager regretfully informed me that I could no longer be in the kitchen.

However, as I entered my teens, my perspective shifted dramatically. I became increasingly embarrassed by your grandfather's profession. When classmates spoke proudly of their fathers' office jobs, I'd mumble, "My father works in a kitchen," their laughter lingering in my mind. I began to view his job as menial and our financial struggles as evidence of his inadequacy. The rich experiences and sacrifices that had once defined my world now seemed inadequate against my narrow definition of success.

For years, I resented your grandfather's lack of formal education, blaming him for not guiding us more effectively. I was frustrated that he couldn't help me with my studies or understand the world

I was growing up in. His limited English and modest reading habits only seemed to reinforce my misguided sense of superiority.

Ironically, my own education was far from ideal. Many of my school teachers struggled with English, often reciting textbook knowledge without truly understanding it themselves. I gained little from their instruction, a reality that would haunt me in the years to come.

It took a long time for me to appreciate the skills and wisdom your grandfather possessed. Eight years after being banned from the hotel kitchen, I returned as an apprentice to that very same place, retracing the path I had once dismissed with disdain. This return marked the beginning of a profound realization of my identity and roots.

As I delved deeper into the world I had previously shunned, I began to understand a fundamental truth: running away from one's identity doesn't lead to fulfillment. I had spent years pretending, desperately trying to mold myself into something I was not, hoping for acceptance. But no matter how much I tried to distance myself from my heritage, the world saw me as I truly was. My attempts to escape my roots left me feeling hollow, disconnected from both the world I aspired to and the one I came from.

5.

When I was about 14, major riots erupted in Bangalore, once again, over the Cauvery River dispute. These riots raged for over two months, plunging the city into chaos and fear. The once-bustling streets became eerily deserted. Burnt-out buses stood as grim reminders of the violence, while abandoned bikes and scooters cluttered the roads, their owners having fled in terror.

Police barricades cropped up at every corner, and the air was thick with the acrid smell of burning petrol and rubber. An undercurrent of tension pulsed through the very pavement beneath our feet.

One day, as I was returning from school with my sister and three neighbor kids, all younger than me, we encountered a scene of chaos—a bus was set ablaze, and people were shouting slogans. Fear gripped us. Suddenly, a group of men on motorbikes, with the flag of Kannada statehood tied to the front, approached. Two of the bikes carried four men each, a clear sign that the rule of law had broken down. They asked us if we were Kannadigas, the natives who spoke the local language, Kannada.

For the first time in years, I didn't want to hide. I felt a compelling urge to be truthful; something inside me shifted. I looked at my sister and our three friends; as the eldest, I knew they were looking to me for guidance. The men on motorbikes waited for an answer. My sister and our three friends looked at me. I took a breath. "We are Tamils," I replied in English. It was probably the most reckless thing I could have done in the midst of a mob, but at that moment, it felt like the right thing to do. I don't know if it was my clear, direct reply or simply the fact that I spoke in English, but they left us alone and rode off, shouting slogans as they went.

That day, I felt an unexpected sense of pride. I hadn't let my sister down or allowed my own insecurities and cultural conflict to dictate my actions. Although I still can't speak or write Tamil well, I haven't denied my identity since that day.

6.

Two years later, another pivotal moment occurred when I applied to a pre-university college. Your grandfather accompanied me to the interview, taking time off from work. Standing in line, I was acutely aware of how different he looked from the other parents. Still, in his work uniform, the aroma of spices clung to his clothes, and stains marked his attire. His feet were shod in simple sandals.

My embarrassment peaked when he lit a beedi—not even a cigarette, but a humble beedi. The strong tobacco smoke filled the air, and despite my repeated pleas for him to wait until we were out of the building, he continued smoking, seemingly unbothered by my discomfort. I knew he had switched from cigarettes to beedis, sacrificing his own comforts to meet our needs, yet I couldn't shake the sense of shame that washed over me. He stood there, unbothered, a man who had worked too hard to care about such things.

In the principal's office, your grandfather stood humbly, refusing to sit despite my urging. The principal gave me a stern look and asked, "Are you not ashamed of yourself?" He pointed out that I had only secured 72 percentage, a score he said was only suitable for the Arts stream—a stream often looked down upon, considered a last resort for those who didn't fit in elsewhere. Then he turned to your grandfather and asked me in English, "What does your father do for a living?"

When I answered, the principal looked at your grandfather for a long, silent moment. Then, with a tone that surprised me, he said, "I'm going to place you in the commerce stream because of your father." Still holding his gaze on my father, he continued, "You are what makes this country great. Here you are, coming straight from work, rushing here for your son. You remind me of my own father, and his father was a farmer."

Your grandfather simply replied, "Thank you, sir. Please look after my son."

That moment forced me to reconsider everything I thought I knew about your grandfather. Outside, he embraced me, saying, "I'm proud of you. You're going to university." There was no mention of my previous behavior, no reprimand—just unconditional love and support.

This was a turning point in my life, but the journey to truly understand your grandfather and his quiet strength was far from over.

7.

A pivotal moment occurred during a summer trip to Mangadu. I would have been 7 years old. I had cried, not wanting to leave your grandfather behind and go ahead with my mother and sisters. Understanding my reluctance, he arranged to bring me along later that night. I spent the evening with him in the kitchen as he worked through his shift. Later, we ended up hitching a ride in a lorry. It was only later that I learned this was how he often traveled—saving money and avoiding the hassle of reservations, as he never had set travel dates. This was normal for him—saving money, making do, finding solutions.

We were dropped off in Vellore at 2 AM, still 40 kilometers from our destination. It was pouring rain. Your grandfather carried me in his arms, wrapping me in a rug to keep me dry, and started searching for transportation. When none could be found, he decided to take shelter under a nearby thatched roof by the bus stop. As we stood there, the roof offering little protection from the relentless downpour, a man opened his door and invited us inside.

The house was tiny—barely one room, dimly lit by an oil lamp with an open fire in the corner serving as the kitchen. The stranger, who had just finished work, was preparing a meal. As I shivered from the cold, your grandfather, without hesitation or invitation, stepped in and took over the cooking. It wasn't something he had to be asked to do; it was simply in his nature. His sudden decision to start cooking in a stranger's home surprised me. The aroma of the food filled the small space, and despite having been half-asleep, I was suddenly wide awake and ravenous. We ended up having a hearty meal that early morning, and by the time we left, your grandfather had made a friend out of the stranger, who then accompanied us to the bus station and saw us off.

Even to this day, I am amazed at the ease with which he could forge a connection with anyone. The way he interacted with the lorry driver, the kind stranger, and everyone we encountered along the way revealed a social grace I had never noticed in him before. He had a unique ability to connect with people from all walks of life, especially those from humble backgrounds. While I sometimes viewed these individuals with a sense of detachment or even disdain, wondering how anyone could engage with them, your grandfather would be right there, sharing a meal and finding common ground.

8.

As I faced my own challenges in life, my perspective on your grandfather continued to evolve. With each twist in my journey, I found myself reflecting on his life, marveling at how he managed to navigate it all.

When I struggled to make ends meet in my first job, I thought of how your grandfather supported our family of seven on a modest income. When I encountered discrimination or hardship, I remembered how he faced a world that often belittled him, yet he always maintained his dignity.

Each stage of my life brought new insights into the strength and resilience your grandfather possessed. I came to realize the arrogance in expecting him to help with studies he never had the opportunity to pursue. His unwavering commitment to our education, despite his own limited schooling, spoke volumes about his wisdom and the dreams he held for us.

Isha, I share this with you because I want you to understand the complex layers of our relationships with parents, culture, and identity. The anger and shame I felt as a child eventually transformed into deep respect and love for your grandfather and our heritage. But beyond that, I want you to learn from my mistakes.

Your journey of identity will likely be even more complex than mine. Growing up in Australia with a Tamil father and a Tulu-speaking mother, you are immersed in a mix of cultures. At home, we mostly speak English, but you're surrounded by fragments of other traditions—my Tamil programs and music, my love for cricket, and my unwavering support for the Indian cricket team.

Your mother, culturally Australian, has her own unique habits and traditions. She eats beef and pork, which I abstain from—not just because of my cultural beliefs but also because I'm not accustomed to their taste and flavor. This may seem like a small detail, but it highlights the broader spectrum of differences and similarities that shape our family life. Our meals are a blend of Tamil vegetarian dishes and your mother's Australian favorites.

These differences might sometimes feel confusing or even conflicting, but they also create a rich mosaic of experiences and perspectives. You get to witness how diverse traditions and beliefs can coexist within a single family, teaching you the value of tolerance and understanding.

As you grow, you'll find yourself navigating multiple identities—Australian, Indian, Tamil, Tulu. Each one is an essential thread in the fabric of who you are. This diverse background is not a challenge to be overcome but a strength to be embraced. It offers you a unique perspective and a broader understanding of the world.

You may feel pulled in different directions at times or struggle to find where you fit. But remember, these diverse identities are not a burden—they are a source of strength. Embracing them will give you a richer, more nuanced view of life and the ability to connect with people from all walks of life.

You were born to migrant parents, just as I was. However, Australia, your home, isn't as divided or polarized by language as India was during my youth. Still, you'll face your own unique challenges. My advice to you is to fully integrate into this wonderful country that has welcomed us. Embrace its values, opportunities, and way of life. At the same time, cherish the rich cultural heritage you come from. Your background is a gift, offering insights and perspectives that can enrich both your life and the lives of those around you. Find a balance between honoring your roots and planting new ones on Australian soil. This duality isn't a weakness; it's a strength that will help you navigate our increasingly interconnected world.

When you see anyone on the street—a beggar, someone homeless—or when you interact with a waiter, a taxi driver, a chef, or someone serving food in a restaurant or working in retail, remember that your grandfather and your father did similar work. Every person you encounter has a story, a journey that brought them to where they are. They deserve your respect, regardless of their job or status.

We often think too highly of ourselves and overlook the paths our parents and others have walked before us. Your grandfather's life, with all its struggles and triumphs, is a testament to the dignity of hard work and perseverance. It's a part of your story, too.

As you grow, I hope you'll carry these lessons with you. Treat everyone with respect, knowing that each person's journey is unique and valuable. Remember that understanding often comes with time and reflection. The people we might dismiss in our youth may become those we admire most as we gain wisdom.

Embrace the richness of your heritage, Isha. It holds the strength and wisdom of generations before you. Your journey of self-discovery won't always be easy, but it will be deeply meaningful. You have a unique gift to bridge worlds and understand perspectives shaped by the cultures that define our family. When I visit India, I still touch your grandfather's watches, his leather jacket, his belt, and his glasses. Fourteen years have passed since he left us, yet the house carries pieces of him—a quiet reminder of his presence and all he did for us. And through you, his story continues.

I miss him. I miss my dad.

If a man can make his son sit up at night, think of him, dream of him, and miss him, then in all accounts, that man has been a good dad. I hope you will remember me as a good dad, too.

I'm sorry, Isha.

I say sorry because I feel I owe you one—not just for the things I've done, but for the things I failed to consider. For the moments I thought leaving was the right thing, not thinking about what that might have done to you. For believing that cutting short and walking away would somehow make things easier, when in reality, it might have left shadows I never meant for you to carry.

But know this—I will be here for you. No matter what.

I wonder, Isha—how will you hold all the pieces of yourself when they feel like they belong to different worlds? When parts of your identity seem to pull in different directions, will you see them as a conflict or as a gift? Will you embrace them as I eventually did, or will you struggle, as I once did, before realizing that home isn't one place, one language, or one story—it's something we build with those we love?

And when you think of me years from now, what will you remember? What pieces of me will you carry forward, and what will you choose to leave behind?

What will stay? What will you let go of?

With all my love,

Your Appā

What Love Taught Me

As you grow, you'll meet many people. Some will catch your eye, others will capture your interest, and a precious one may steal your heart. This is natural, beautiful, and an essential part of the human experience.

But I want you to understand something crucial: being in love is far more complex than movies or songs would have you believe. It's a kaleidoscope of emotions viewed through the prism of your own experiences, family influences, and societal expectations. Love isn't just what you feel; it's what you choose to nurture, build, and sometimes fight for.

I've been in love a few times in my life. I have a smile on my face when I say 'a few times', knowing well that's a lie, but I will leave it as is. Each experience was unique, and each taught me something different. It's only with time and reflection that I've begun to truly appreciate the nuances of love, to understand its beauty and its burdens. Love is both fragile and resilient, capable of being tested in ways you can't yet imagine.

Don't strain yourself trying to define or fully comprehend love. It's enough to know that it's complex, that it differs for everyone, and that there's no one-size-fits-all definition or understanding of it.

What I can share with you are the experiences that I've gathered along the way. Take what resonates with you, and know that your journey will be uniquely yours.

If I asked you about love, you might recite poetry, talk about first kisses, butterflies. But you can't know the complexity of loving someone deeply while also resenting them, of being bound to a person by commitment and shared history even as you feel yourself drifting further apart. You haven't yet seen how love grows, shifts, and sometimes cracks under the weight of life.

You think you understand love, but there's a world of difference between observing life and living it. The weight of years presses down on a relationship, slowly transforming passion into routine. You haven't experienced how love evolves, from the initial rush of passion to a steady companionship and, sometimes, to a burden you carry silently.

You haven't felt the subtle shift when conversations that once flowed freely become stilted and forced. You don't know the ache of lying beside someone who feels miles away, even as they sleep next to you. Or worse, the hollow feeling when they choose to sleep in another room, unable to bear your presence.

You don't yet understand how the world outside can seep into your private space, how societal expectations and family pressures can strain even the strongest bonds. You haven't faced the challenge of forgiving someone you love for hurting you deeply, only to find that forgiveness doesn't erase the memory of the pain. You'll come to see that forgiveness isn't a cure—it's a decision to move forward with the scars intact.

You haven't lived through the nights one spends eating dinner alone, the TV's glow his only company, or the evenings one passes listening to his own writings echo in an empty house. You haven't yet felt the pain of enduring silence, the kind that presses heavily against your chest, knowing you're holding on for someone else's sake, not your own.

Financial hardships are more than just numbers on paper. You haven't felt the cold grip of humiliation when you realize you've lost everything—not just money, but respect, dignity, and your sense of self. You haven't seen that look in your partner's eyes—a mix of disappointment, resentment, and pity—that cuts deeper than any words could. As financial strain seeps into every aspect of life, it transforms even the most mundane moments. Breakfast tables become battlefields, where the conversation in the house drops down to a few sentences a day, and when something is spoken, it's mostly about you or about who is taking the car to work; you don't know the pain when your wife casually mentions changing all her passwords, casually!! and you're too afraid to ask for the new ones—that's when you know it's not love anymore, but an agreed connection serving emotional needs for the time being.

Love isn't just poetry or promises; it's the quiet decision to stay, even when every fiber of your being tells you to leave. It's the courage to face another day together when everything feels broken. You don't know what it's like to love someone deeply while simultaneously wondering if you even know them anymore.

You haven't felt the gradual erosion of your individual identity, the slow blending into a 'we' that sometimes leaves you wondering who 'I' really is. You don't know how memories can be both a comfort and a torment, how a song or a place can flood you with nostalgia one moment and regret the next.

You don't know the pain when she asks if you have ever cheated on her in the middle of kissing; no sonnets or lines from my own poetry will ever truly convey how deep these scars run.

You haven't experienced the silent wars fought around kitchen sinks, seated on dining tables, the unspoken tensions that fill a room more densely than any argument could. You haven't yet learned how true intimacy requires courage that goes beyond any physical act, the bravery it takes to lay your soul bare before another.

You haven't stood at the edge of despair, staring into nothing, thinking—maybe it's easier to just go. Contemplating an end to it all, only to be pulled back because of a small hand holding yours, his daughter's innocent laughter. You won't know what it feels like to be told that your daughter is weak and needs special care and then to sit next to her, holding her hands, watching her sleep, and praying to any god who might be listening. You don't know the anguish of seeing your child without the strength to drink those two spoons of milk, tears rolling down your face and falling on her forehead.

I'm telling you this not to discourage you but to prepare you.

Love is a blessing that decides to stay or leave of its own accord. Nothing you do can force it to stay, but your actions can certainly hasten its exit. It's a feeling that ties you to a destiny, either in hell or heaven. But love is also where hope lives—where, even in the darkest moments, a small light can pull you forward.

You are that light, Isha. Through all the heartbreaks, you are my constant, my reason to stay.

When I hold your hand, when I hear your laughter, I remember what love can be at its purest. A bond that doesn't ask. Doesn't falter. Just is.

I wonder, Isha—will love be something that reshapes you, or will it be something you shape yourself? Will it bring you closer to who you are, or will it demand that you become someone you never thought you would be? And when it reveals parts of yourself you weren't prepared to see—will you have the courage to face them?

Because love is many things, Isha. But easy is never one of them.

Appā

Life on Both Sides of the Line

Dear Isha,

It was summer. We were at Nan's house in Mangadu, our usual holiday escape from the city. Free of school work and schedules—just days that stretched out filled with the kind of freedom only childhood summers can bring. The summer was hot, as usual. The clay-rich red soil cracked under the sun. My sisters and I spent hours in the small canals between the paddy, under the shade of toddy palm trees, catching tadpoles, chasing crabs disappearing into mud holes. Life moved differently in the village compared to Bangalore—bare feet kicking up mud, the kind that sticks and doesn't wash off until you've scrubbed three times. Nan was out there too, crouched low, picking brinjals, sorting through green chilies, doing whatever needed doing in the field.

We heard loud shouts coming from the direction of the well. The wells in the fields were just circular mouths in the ground with no walls or fences used for irrigation. The sound wasn't panicked, but it carried an urgency that made us freeze. Our mother and Nan always told us to stay away from them. In a place where life moved slowly, the sight of people running stirred an unfamiliar fear. The shouting softened, but a crowd had gathered. We weren't used to seeing so many people running, and the confusion scared us. We didn't know what to do, so we ran to Nan. She told us that a cow or a goat might have fallen into the well, and she was right. "It's bad luck when a cow dies on your land," she told us. She clicked her tongue, murmuring that a cow had probably fallen in, and I could see the worry on her face as she whispered, "Bad luck. Hard times might follow for that family." She then said a prayer that nothing terrible should come upon the family who owned the well. I overheard people whispering that if the cow wasn't removed quickly, the water would be undrinkable for weeks. My sisters, scared by all this, ran back to the house. I didn't want to leave; I wanted to watch the spectacle. I remember feeling a strange pull I couldn't explain—a compulsion to see what was happening.

The whispers around us confirmed it—a cow had indeed fallen into the well. Someone called out, "Send word to the Paracheri! The Paraiyars need to come and help pull it out." As we waited, I heard someone remark, "A feast for the Paracheri today," and another responded with a quiet, "So unfair."

And then I saw them—the Paraiyars—arriving with a long wooden pole. They were men of tall frames, their skin darkened by the sun, wearing only lungis and thin cloths tied around their waists. They came in a respectful, bowed-down stance, yet I noticed a small smile on their faces. To my young mind, their quiet smiles seemed out of place, almost wrong in the face of what felt like tragedy. I looked around, searching for answers on the faces of those around me, but all I saw was a quiet acceptance, as though each reaction was expected. It was my first inkling of the invisible lines that divided us, lines I hadn't yet seen but somehow felt.

And then, after 30 minutes or so, they pulled the cow, which was dead, out of the well. The sight of the cow's lifeless body being pulled up from the well, limp and heavy, felt like a punch. I had never seen death before. The cow's eyes, open but empty, were haunting, and as I watched the men tie it to a pole. I was even more shocked when they hoisted it onto their shoulders, and when they walked, they were smiling and glancing at each other in quiet joy. I watched as they carried it through the field, along the main road, past the Ganesha temple, and toward the river. The contrast rattled me. How could death bring smiles?

I reached for my friend and whispered, "What are they going to do with the cow?"

He didn't even look at me. "They'll take it back to the Paracheri, and they're going to eat it."

The words hit me like a betrayal, tearing through everything I thought I knew. A cow wasn't food; it was sacred, a quiet member of our fields. I looked at the men, wondering what they saw that we didn't.

"What?" I exclaimed, my voice trembling. I had never heard of such a thing before. We weren't big meat eaters—our meals were simple: rice, lentils, vegetables, and occasionally chicken or eggs on Sundays being the extent of our indulgence. The idea of eating a cow felt not just unfamiliar but like a breach of everything I knew about what was right and wrong.

This moment lingered in my mind. I couldn't understand why everyone seemed to have a different reaction. To one group, it was a matter of celebration—a feast to look forward to. I saw the smiles on their faces and heard the quiet murmurs, and it felt wrong like joy shouldn't belong in a moment like this. To others, it was jealousy—watching someone else's gain. 'Look at them, smiling,' I overheard one man mutter. But for the people whose well the cow had fallen into, it was different. I could see the worry in their eyes. I felt their fear, too, even though I didn't understand it fully then. To them, it wasn't just a dead cow—it was a sign of the hard times that lay ahead. I had never encountered death before, and the reactions around me—some celebrating, others resentful, and some worried about the bad luck it brought—added layers of confusion.

It was a reminder that even in a small village, there were vast differences in how people lived and what they believed. But eating cow meat wasn't something I had ever imagined.

The cow incident left me with questions I couldn't shake. The paraiyars were all I could think and talk about that day. That night, as we sat in the veranda, Nan must have noticed our conversation that day. She called us over. She was busy with her betel nut-crushing. "Don't worry," she said. "They mean no harm". She didn't look up as she spoke. Her hands slowed their steady crush of betel nuts, eyes cast down as if unwilling to meet mine, yet firm in her words: 'They're not like us," her voice softer now. Her words hung in the air, a caution wrapped in reassurance. Her words were meant to reassure me, but they only confused me more.

I was scared to ask Nan more about the Paraiyars and the paracheri; the fear had settled deep within me. The only person I could think of that I could ask was my friend Ram. He was my holiday friend. Unlike me, the annual visitor to Mangadu, he had never ventured out of Mangadu, and he knew every corner of the village. Ram introduced me to a world beyond the compound walls of the five-star hotel I was used to in Bangalore. He showed me how to play marbles, the art of spinning tops, and the joy of running barefoot through paddy fields. We explored Mangadu together—he was like a Huckleberry Finn to me, and I adored his freedom and spirit.

I asked Ram, my voice dropping to a whisper when I mentioned the paracheri. He shrugged, pointing casually beyond the temple as if it were just another direction, not a world divided from ours.

"They live there. We don't go," he said like it was the simplest thing in the world.

But the way his eyes darted past mine, avoiding my gaze, made me wonder if he was hiding something—something I wasn't meant to understand. Maybe it was a magical place, like the stories Nan told about hidden treasures or enchanted groves. Maybe it was filled with secrets only the grown-ups knew. The idea of being kept out felt unfair, and I wasn't in the mood to accept it. This time, I stood my ground and asked again, my voice firm.

'Show me where the paracheri is,' I demanded, feeling a thrill run through me as if I was daring to unlock a secret everyone else wanted to keep hidden. Each step felt like an act of defiance, a small rebellion against a world that seemed too eager to stay hidden. I was only a child, yet it felt as though I was on the edge of something vast and forbidden.

Ram then raced through the paddy fields; I chased him, mud splashing as we ran. He always knew where the best hiding spots were, leading me to corners of Mangadu I had never seen.

To me, he was more than just a friend: he was a guide to a world I didn't fully understand, one that I was desperate to explore.

"There," he said, pointing past the Ganesha temple, past the stream where women washed clothes on flat rocks, past our lands, and even past the Sivan temple. That temple was known for spirits and dark forces; we always stayed far from it. I could feel that the air was warmer, filled with the smell of what seemed to be the smoke of them cooking various animals and distant voices, a world that felt both near and unreachable.

Ram's voice lowered, "That's the Paracheri." He spoke it like a fact, not a mystery. "They live there. We don't go," he added. His tone was casual. "We don't go to Paracheri, and they weren't supposed to spend the night in our village." I wondered if he was hiding something, if he, too, felt the pull of the unknown.

This "us" and "them" dynamic was confusing. In the simplicity of childhood, it felt unfair. Why couldn't we go there? Why couldn't they stay here? I asked him. He explained to me that it was how things were. The 'us'—the farmers, the villagers who worked the fields and stayed within the village—and 'them'—those from the paracheri who took on the jobs we didn't. There was an unspoken agreement, a line neither side crossed. But these boundaries confused me. Why did 'us' and 'them' even matter if we all lived under the same sky?

Mangadu was just one of the hundreds of villages that existed in my part of the world, growing up, that had the caste lines drawn so clearly that they became invisible, like air—something everyone breathed in without question.

As a child, I accepted that the Paraiyars lived beyond the temples and the streams and that our paths rarely crossed. I believed, without question, that this was just the way things were. But looking back, I realize how much these boundaries controlled our lives. The people from the paracheri weren't allowed to cross into our world, but we depended on them for work no one else would do—fixing roofs, chopping wood, and working in the fields. I grew up seeing them as both essential and invisible.

One evening, Ram and I were taking a dip in the canal near the Sivan temple when he pointed at the paracheri and a funeral procession heading to the river for cremation.

"It's from the Paracheri," Ram whispered.

I turned to him, startled. I hadn't imagined that they used the same riverbank as us.

"They use the same riverbank as us?" I asked, disbelief clear in my voice.

Ram shrugged slightly, not meeting my eyes. "Where else would they go?" he said.

We watched silently as they carried the body to the river. There was no chanting, no priests. Their rituals seemed simpler and quieter. I froze, startled. I had never seen a dead body before, and the sight of death—so stark and unhidden—shook me. The quiet finality of it all, following so quickly after the cow's death, was too much. My chest tightened, and my legs moved before I could think. I turned and ran, leaving Ram behind as I raced home, my heart pounding with a mix of fear and confusion.

I couldn't take my mind away from it. I had imagined their world as something completely different from ours—a place filled with shadows and unfamiliar shapes, far removed from our familiar village lanes. But watching the funeral procession from the paracheri, I felt an odd sense of connection. The same riverbank where my family's rituals were performed held their grief, too. The separation that felt so wide during life seemed to narrow in death. But even as I felt this closeness, I pulled back, unsure if I was allowed or supposed to feel this odd kinship with 'them.'

I was surprised that they used the same riverbanks as 'us' in the village, but it was too much for me to process. The funeral procession was an odd sight. Despite the separation in life, in death, both 'us' and 'them' ended up on the same riverbank for cremation. Our paths to the river were different, but the resting ground was the same.

It was the first time I felt the blurred lines between "us" and "them." In life, the separation seemed vast; in death, it narrowed. The realization left me unsettled. Was death the only place where these boundaries dissolved?

It felt like a contradiction, one that echoed the blurred lines I was beginning to see in our small village. The division felt both artificial and deeply embedded. It was too much for me to process.

Quiet lessons of Nan

At home, the divide was subtler but ever-present. The Paraiyars came to work in our fields and homes. They worked for money, food, or both. Sometimes, they would come to our house to do work around the house. When they finished, my mother would often give them food or leftovers. The men would, therefore, usually sit around, lighting beedis, smoke curling in the evening light as their children and women pack what my mother had to give. My Nan didn't like them hanging around the house after work. She had a way of saying things without saying them. But after they left, Nan would pour water over where they had sat and would sweep the place thoroughly. It was a routine gesture, her way of keeping things as they were, a ritual passed down. It was as if her hands followed a path laid down by generations before her, a routine so familiar she didn't need to explain. But each splash of water planted a seed in me, teaching me without words that boundaries weren't just physical—they were rituals, habits, and inherited ways of being. At the time, I thought it was just one of Nan's quirks, like the prayers she muttered over our meals. But each splash of water was a lesson; she redrew the lines that divided our worlds, teaching me that some spaces were never meant to be shared.

I never questioned it then; I thought it was just something Nan did. But now I realize it was her way of maintaining the boundary between us and them, a line she drew with every splash of water. Her gestures, her quiet comments about keeping our space clean, all planted seeds in me—seeds that told me there was something different, something 'less' about those who lived beyond the stream.

In the evenings, as we sat outside or played in the courtyard after the sun had set and the air had cooled, we'd always see a herd of pigs and piglets walking past our house, herded by men returning them home after a day of grazing. The pigs ate anything they found along the way, and it was a delight to watch. One day, knowing my interest, Ram told me that the men herding them were parayans.

From then on, I started noticing the herders more closely. They were dark-skinned, often shirtless, and looked like the men who had pulled the cow out of the well. I would stand and stare at them, creating stories in my mind about their lives, homes, and children—a world far from ours, beyond the lines drawn by the village.

Even after all these years, I can still feel the weight of those childhood questions. Why did "us" and "them" matter so much? Why were their lives considered less, their presence seen as something to erase after they left?

The Paracheri wasn't just a place beyond the stream—it was a world of people whose work we relied on yet whose existence we kept at a distance. They were both essential and invisible. And the contradictions of that dynamic stayed with me long after the summers in Mangadu were over.

The pigs, the funeral processions, the whispered warnings—all of it painted a picture of a world where divisions were so deeply ingrained that they went unquestioned. But as a child, I did question them. And those questions have shaped how I see the world now.

2.

Back in Bangalore, the distinction between "us" and "them" wasn't as clear-cut. People of all colors and backgrounds lived in the city, and the lines weren't as simple. But my mother had an eye for detail. If she sensed visitors were Paraiyars, she would make sure to track what they touched and where they sat. It wasn't as straightforward as it had been in the village, where the boundaries were explicit.

By the time I reached college, I had begun to understand the weight of these distinctions. We were all the same, and the hierarchy imposed by a society steeped in stigma and superstition was not something I could accept. But the truth is, even though caste faded into the background, a new marker took its place—money. The hierarchy was different, with money replacing caste as the marker.

In Bangalore, we lived in a one-room house—a small, shared space where every corner carried the weight of modest means. There was poverty, but as a child, I didn't fully grasp it. What I did notice, however, was the scrutiny. We weren't asked about our caste, but eyes lingered on our belongings as though silently tallying our place based on what we owned. I sensed it in the way people looked at our small space when they visited, the clothes we wore, and how we lived our lives. It wasn't outright discrimination, but there was a kind of judgment—an unspoken awareness of where we stood.

We were at the bottom of both ladders, feeling the weight of the gaze from others who seemed to have climbed higher. I realized then that lines weren't just etched in caste; they shifted, bending around status and wealth—a hierarchy that evolved yet remained just as sharp. I've seen the pain those lines cause.

Though caste may have faded, its shadow lingered. Even in cities like Bangalore, where diversity seemed to mask divisions, it didn't take much for those lines to surface. A normal conversation would often start with a seemingly innocent question: "Where are you from?" It sounded harmless, but then the probing began, slowly revealing where you stood. The name of your street would become a verdict. Temple Street, Merchant Street, Market Street, Station Street—those names got a nod of approval. Anything else meant you were on the fringes. Grown men are brought to tears when arranging marriages for their children. It didn't matter how much they had worked to build a life, to climb that ladder—they knew that one question about the street they came from could undo decades of effort. It was like a stain that didn't wash off, always lingering beneath the surface. And when the next generation was ready to start a family, those old classifications would resurface, dragging everything back into the light. It's a weight that never truly lifts. It wasn't just history—it was inheritance.

When I moved to Australia, I was in awe of what I saw. The expanse, the openness—it felt like the boundaries I had grown up with were being redrawn. I am still in awe of how beautiful this country is. This country has been good to me. It accepted me, gave me an opportunity, and I took on this land as my home. I consider myself part of this land now. But I thought the lines would fade here, that the diversity would erase the boundaries I'd known. It didn't take long, though, to realize they just took new forms. I was naive to think the lines would vanish. They didn't. They just changed shape.

One night, still new to this country, I was walking down Chapel Street after dinner and someone called me a 'boong.' I didn't know what it meant, but the way it was said—and the laughter that followed—told me enough. There were harsher moments, too— being told to 'get out of this country,' called 'tax scum,' and accused of 'living off the dole.' These words weren't just slurs— they were weapons, sharpened by fear and wielded by those desperate to protect their lines.

I've felt this hostility in smaller ways, too. I've seen anger shown toward me at checkout counters or while standing in line to order food or waiting for the bus. A few times, I've been ignored altogether, asked to repeat even simple words, or only attended to when I made it a point to complain. I know my H's don't always sound the way they expect, and my V's might come across as a B. But that shouldn't matter. When it happens, I tell myself it's their problem, not mine. I have felt this before, in Singapore too, when taxi drivers would refuse to take me on some nights while they accepted the same fare from my white friends. It's the dirt in their heart; I have other things to worry about.

Discrimination finds a way; it doesn't disappear; it evolves. Be it Mangadu, Bangalore, Hong Kong, Singapore, or even Sydney—it just wears different clothes. Here in Australia, it speaks better English, but the meaning is the same. These moments haven't spoiled my respect for this country. They're reminders that the lines may blur, but they don't disappear. And so, I move forward, carrying both the beauty and the weight of this place I now call home.

3.

You started playschool. You were just four, and you had a good group of friends. You would come home every day, your face bright as you talked about Sydney, Isabella, Taco, and all the games you played. I could hear the joy in your voice, and it felt like everything was right in your small world.

Then one day, you came back quiet, your eyes downcast. You told me three girls wouldn't let you into the cubby house because you were dark. I saw the sadness in your eyes, and it wasn't just sadness—it was confusion. You couldn't understand why you were left out.

It wasn't just a locked cubby house. You began asking me about the color of your skin and why it was different. Your voice—small and hesitant—cut through me. 'Why is my skin darker?' you asked, your voice a whisper, almost like you were afraid of the answer. In that moment, I wanted to shield you from the weight of that question, to erase the lines that had once made me feel small. But how could I protect you from something even I couldn't see? Her small voice asking about her skin brought me back to the edge of the stream in Mangadu, standing with Ram, looking toward the paracheri. I had no answers then, and I had none now. But the same feeling settled in my chest—a weight, a sense of something unfair and unchangeable.

My response—that we are all different and that you were too good for them—felt like sand slipping through my fingers. I knew my reply wasn't enough. I told you we were all special in our own ways and encouraged you to find other friends to play other games. But I could see it didn't make sense to you. I watched you push your food around on your plate, your shoulders hunched, and I knew my words hadn't reached you.

The sadness of the cubby house seemed to follow you. You started asking me questions—at the park, during swimming lessons—each time you noticed that you were different. 'Why is my skin darker?' you asked, your voice so small it almost broke me. You started noticing the shades of other kids' skin, and when you were around other South Indian children with skin darker than yours or your own, you seemed both surprised and comforted. It pained me deeply that you had to find solace in such a way that the questions had already begun to weigh on you at such a young age.

And each time, it left a mark. You began asking the same question to your grandparents as well. You became quieter, the questions piling up as if you were carrying a weight too heavy for your small shoulders. I wanted to take it up with the daycare center, but your mother asked me not to. It's not the center; it was the kids.

The sadness of the cubby house seemed to follow you, echoing in the questions you began to ask—at the park, during swimming lessons—each time you noticed that you were different.

The questions began. 'Why is my skin darker?' you asked, voice small, eyes searching.

I wanted to tell you it didn't matter. But I knew it did.

On your graduation day from daycare, I carried you around the classroom as you proudly showed me every corner of your world—art projects, cubbies, the small kitchen. Then we came to the cubby house. Though you had long since moved on from it, I stood by its door, feeling the helplessness I'd once felt as a child, watching lines drawn in the mud of Mangadu. It was as though those lines had followed us here, invisible but no less sharp, waiting to box you out as they had once boxed out others.

Back then, the boundaries in Mangadu were mapped out clearly—past temples, beyond streams. Here, they hid behind locked cubby house doors or whispered words. As a child, I accepted those lines without question. It wasn't until I saw you struggle with these invisible boundaries that I began to revisit my own childhood. The lines that once felt so fixed in Mangadu now seemed arbitrary, just like the borders I saw being drawn around you.

Isha, I've stood on both sides of those lines. I've watched water poured to erase footprints in Mangadu. I've had words thrown at me for my skin, my accent, my place in this world.

These lines—no matter how solid they seem—are only as permanent as we allow them to be.

Some nights, I lie awake thinking about that cow in the well. About the men carrying it away. About seven-year-old me, scared of the people past the temples. About four-year-old you, trying to understand why a cubby house has borders. It's a weight we both carry, but it doesn't have to be ours forever.

Boundaries, Isha, are always drawn by someone. By hands, by rules, by history, by fear. But that doesn't mean they're real. They're only as solid as we let them be.

Your friends may come around, or they may not. The mutterers will keep muttering. That's their burden to carry, not yours. Let them draw their lines. We'll be too busy living, too free to notice their boundaries.

I wonder, Isha—have invisible boundaries shaped the way you see the world or yourself? Have you ever questioned the lines drawn between people? And when you do—when you stand at the edge of a boundary someone else has drawn—will you accept it, or will you step past it?

Love, Appā

The Cubby House

Isha,

When you asked me why your skin was darker and why others sometimes treated you differently, I gave you the best answer I could at that moment: "We are all different, and that's what makes us special." But I saw in your eyes that my words didn't land. You didn't believe me, and I understand why. It felt like I was brushing your questions aside, but the truth is, I wasn't. I know this pain intimately, and I have walked this path before you.

When I was your age, I didn't just notice my skin—I was told it was something to notice. I was the darkest in my class, and Tamil on top of that. The city I grew up in had tensions around Tamil identity because of the ongoing dispute over the Cauvery River. Those two parts of me—my skin and my Tamil heritage—became targets for the cruel remarks that children can hurl without fully understanding their impact.

I remember the day it became undeniable. A boy on the playground refused to play with me. You're dark,' he said, 'so you must be dirty.' His words didn't just sting—they spread. By the end of the day, my friends, the ones I sat next to every day, were calling me "blackie." I didn't know what I had done to deserve it. I cried alone, a boy suddenly isolated in the world that had once felt safe. When I asked my mother about it, she brushed it off, maybe because she didn't know what to say, just as I struggled when you asked me.

I cried that day, sitting alone, not knowing who to turn to. When I asked my mother about it, she didn't take much notice. Maybe she didn't know what to say, just like I didn't know what to tell you. For a ten-year-old who sees the classroom and playground as his entire world, this was segregation in every sense of the word. I felt as though a line had been drawn, one that I couldn't cross, one that told me I wasn't enough.

"What made it worse? I found comfort in someone else's misfortune. I saw a boy in another class who was darker than me, and for a moment, I felt relief. At least I'm not him. Even now, it stings to admit that. Because in that moment, I was no different from those who had mocked me."

I had internalized their standards, and in doing so, I perpetuated the same judgment that had hurt me. I wonder if, had I been fairer, I would have done the same to someone darker than me.

But that was the beginning of my journey. It wasn't the end.

Years later, in high school, a boy tried to impress some girls by calling me a crow, mocking me for the color of my skin. He even made crow noises, thinking it was funny. The girls didn't laugh. They didn't find it funny.

Later, some of them came over to apologize. It was a small gesture, but it left a mark. I wondered if their apology came from kindness or from a place of necessity—they often needed my help with studies and tests. Either way, it reminded me that even when people hurt you, there's a chance for redemption.

Still, the internal dialogue was the hardest battle. For years, I prayed for fairer skin. I would ask your grandmother if there was anything I could do to make myself lighter. I tried scrubbing my skin with a clay brick in the shower, thinking it might reveal a fairer layer underneath. It was painful, and when I realized it wouldn't work, I let it go. But the thought lingered. I would have given anything to be a few shades lighter to stop feeling like I didn't belong.

The turning point came in university. One afternoon, sitting in a classroom, I began writing. Inspired by Julius Caesar, I scribbled seven pages of verse about my life—how I felt adrift, with no goalpost to guide me.

But as I wrote, I found something else:

I had found a voice.

The words poured out of me, raw and unfiltered, and when I ran out of paper, I stopped. I sat there, staring at those seven pages, and for the first time, I felt like I could be something. I didn't need anyone's approval or validation. The way I looked didn't define me. It wasn't the external voices that had held me back—it was my own.

I stopped telling myself that being dark was less desirable. I stopped defining myself by someone else's standards. I realized that the power to shape my life and my identity lay within me. And when I started to see myself differently, the world began to look different, too.

But Isha, the world doesn't change overnight. Casual remarks still find their way in, often disguised as jokes. "Smile so we can see you in the dark."

"Why don't you try some fairness cream?"

Some think they're harmless. They're not. They accumulate. They chip away at belonging, little by little, until you start questioning yourself. The world will always have people who measure others by shallow standards. What matters is that you don't let their words shape how you see yourself.

When I tell you that the power to define yourself lies with you, I'm not speaking in abstractions. I'm telling you what I've lived. I've been where you are—questioning, hurting, wondering why the world feels unkind. And I've come out of it stronger. It's not easy, and it doesn't happen all at once. But it starts with changing the voice inside you, with telling yourself that you are enough, just as you are.

You will face moments when the world feels heavy, when the jokes don't feel harmless, and when the questions feel relentless. But know this: the problem isn't you. It's them. Their words reflect their own insecurities, their own limitations, not yours.

You are my daughter, and you carry within you a legacy of resilience.

Our ancestors endured lines drawn in the mud of villages, segregation that shaped lives and futures. Today, those lines may look different, but they still exist.

What matters is how you rise above them.

When I was your age, I wanted to be lighter. But today, I see my skin as a part of my story—a story of resilience, growth, and pride.

Your skin is a part of your story, too, Isha—one that speaks of strength, beauty, and boundless potential. The world will try to define you, to tell you who you are and where you belong. But the only voice that matters, the only one that should ever define you, is your own. And I hope, when you look at yourself, you see what I see: a girl who is more than enough, exactly as she is.

I wonder, Isha, what parts of yourself have you struggled to accept? And how will you begin to see their value—not through someone else's eyes, but your own? Have you ever let someone else's opinion define you? How can you take back that power, shaping your own story instead of letting others write it for you?

Never let the world tell you otherwise. You are enough, exactly as you are. Love, Appā

Karma

Dear Isha,

There's something important I want you to understand about the world we live in—it's a place of balance. Every action we take, every choice we make, sets something in motion. In time, everything falls into place. The people you meet, the moments that feel like déjà vu, the coincidences that make you pause—all of it unfolds when it's meant to. Time is the quiet architect of our lives, bringing together what we need, even when we don't see it in the moment. And when it does, I've come to believe that what we bring to the world—our intentions, being honest to ourselves—shapes what comes back to us. It's not just about what we do—it's about who we are when we do it. That's the part we control. Every choice sends something into motion, even if we don't always see it coming back. Some call it Karma. To me, it's the law of balance—ensuring that everything finds its way, though not always in the ways we expect.

Whether we notice it or not, these choices have a way of coming back to us. This is what people often refer to as Karma—what I see as a law that governs everything, ensuring balance, even if it's not always in the ways we expect. It's a belief that resonates with me, though I've questioned it many times, testing its truth in the light of my own failures and triumphs. Karma isn't just what we choose but sometimes what we inherit or stumble into without realizing it. It reminds us that our actions, whether big or small, weave into the lives around us.

I've mentioned before about my travels after your grandfather passed away in 2008. It was a time when I found myself searching for something—perhaps understanding or maybe just a way to make sense of everything. I was heading to Velankanni, passing through Trichy on a government bus. Retracing his footsteps, thinking like him, visiting the shops and eateries, and staying in the same places he might have—it felt almost therapeutic. Watching the land of the Tamils pass by through the bus window, seeing the graffiti from Dravidian political parties, the billboards with Rajinikanth's larger-than-life face, and interacting with the incredible people—all of it felt alive, rich with stories. There was no urgency, no destination demanding my attention. I wasn't in a rush to get anywhere; I was simply taking it all in. That journey felt like a pause in my life, a moment to just observe and be present without trying to force any answers.

My uncle decided to join me on this trip. He had been feeling restless at home in Kanchipuram and thought the journey might be a welcome distraction. I appreciated the company, even though there were times when I preferred to travel alone. There's a certain freedom in being alone, to be able to extend or shorten a trip as you wish, wandering at your own pace. Traveling alone gives one that liberty—room to linger in moments or leave when the heart whispers it's time. Sometimes, I'd stay longer in a place if the mood struck me, and other times, I'd cut the trip short and head back to Bangalore to spend time with your grandmother. On a few occasions, I even found myself flying back to Chennai—something your grandfather would never have done, as he wasn't one for flights. But for me, it was my way of processing things in my own time, at my own pace.

During that trip, we found ourselves in a small village about 60 kilometers from Trichy. My uncle mentioned an astrologer, someone who read destinies from ancient nadi leaves. I wasn't sure what to believe, but the idea intrigued me, and at that time, I was searching for anything that might offer answers or clarity.

We walked into the astrologer's modest thatched hut—simple and unremarkable. He was a thin, quiet man, sitting with those dried leaves spread out in front of him. There was nothing mystical about the scene, just a man doing what he had likely done countless times before. He ran his fingers over the brittle leaf, scanning words written centuries ago. Then, without hesitation, he said: 'You will marry twice. And you will lose money.'

He spoke it like a fact. It was as if he was reading my future like a simple statement of fact. His words lingered with me. I didn't know why, but I felt their weight, even before I understood what they truly meant.

My uncle, intrigued after seeing my destiny revealed, decided to have his own Nadi leaves read. The astrologer told him he would live a long life.

That night, as my uncle and I sat cross-legged on the floor with plates of rice and lentils at a roadside eatery, dhaba, meant for truck drivers, we talked about our journey, the future, and the past. It wasn't just a meal—we were reflecting. It felt like the kind of conversation that didn't need resolutions or conclusions, just the warmth of understanding shared between two people. We spoke about the choices we had made and where they had led us. It wasn't a grand or dramatic moment, but a quiet one, where meaning quietly settled into the space between words. These were the moments that truly mattered to me—the quiet ones where reflection happens naturally, without being forced.

At the time, the astrologer's words felt like a promise. But, as life often does, it had other plans. My uncle passed away far earlier than anyone could have predicted. It didn't shake my belief that perhaps our lives are written somewhere, but it did make me question whether destiny is as clear-cut as we often think. How could his future, inscribed on those ancient leaves, be so different from what actually happened? Or perhaps it wasn't wrong, and it was in our reading of them—maybe we simply can't fully know what's ahead of us.

I've thought about that day many times since, and while my understanding of destiny remains uncertain, one thing is clear to me: there's a balance in this universe. Life has its own rhythm, one that doesn't always align with what we expect. Events unfold in ways we can't always predict, leaving us to wonder whether anything is truly preordained. For me, the astrologer's words played out exactly as he said. For my uncle, they didn't. Does that mean there's a flaw in the system of destiny? Or are we just unable to see the whole picture? I'm not sure. Who's to say we're not all part of something bigger, something beyond our understanding? Maybe it's all prewritten, maybe we're in a simulation—who knows? Or maybe it's not about knowing the future but making peace with the present.

I thought a lot about your grandfather. He started gambling to relieve some of the pressure. He wasn't chasing a big lottery win, but I think he found the chase alluring. He believed he could crack the code. He would sit on the bed in the living room, scribbling numbers on scraps of paper and tracking the drawn numbers. It became part of his routine. Each small win was a flicker of hope, each loss a deeper shade of disappointment. He'd spend hours looking for patterns, believing that just three numbers might be enough to ease the burden on him, enough to make life a little easier for the family. Sometimes, he won a small amount, but more often, he lost. And each time he lost, I saw the disappointment weigh heavier on him. It wasn't the money that bothered him—it was the feeling of letting us down, of trying to make things better and failing.

Years later, when I lost money—far more than I could handle—it sent me into a dark place. It wasn't just a loss; it was a shattering. I spiraled, questioning everything. There was a moment when I considered leaving everything behind because the weight of it all felt unbearable. But something kept me going, maybe a sliver of hope or the belief that, somehow, balance would be restored. Or perhaps I was just trying to find an excuse for my mistakes. It was a hard lesson, but that's when I started to think more deeply about Karma—not as some cosmic system of reward and punishment, but as the natural way things come back around, even when it seems impossible. Looking back, I wonder if it wasn't balance I was searching for, but forgiveness—of myself, by myself.

August 2020. My lowest point. I was in the shower, sitting down with the water running, and I cried—loudly but hidden by the sound of the shower. I didn't want anyone to hear. The cry came from a deep place, and as I let it out with my eyes closed, I felt the weight of everything on me. But at the same time, I touched something profound—a glimpse of myself I had forgotten existed. Each time I connected with that point and emerged from it, I felt a strange sense of comfort. My breathing deepened, and for the first time in months, I sensed a flicker of hope.

It wasn't just about the release of tears. That experience shifted my perspective entirely. That vulnerable moment cracked something open within me, a door to a part of myself I hadn't dared to face. I saw something beautiful deep within myself, and it gave me the sense that it was time for renewal. In that instant, I felt like I was shedding my old self.

I came to understand that this winter of darkness had to pass so that the plant within me could grow again, could flower. The weight I carried didn't disappear, but it shifted, making space for something new to take root. Through the pain and the release, I found the space to breathe again.

Since then, I've spent a lot of time retracing my steps, the choices and the mistakes I made, the things I should have seen coming but didn't. Looking back, I see a younger version of myself—naive, reckless, and so certain of my invincibility. It surprises me that I made it this far. It feels like life kept trying to teach me lessons, and I kept stubbornly refusing to learn them. I kept repeating the same mistakes, enduring the same disappointments, betrayals, and losses. Only now, after everything, can I see that life didn't punish me—it insisted on my growth.

If life had been gentle, I would have brushed its lessons aside, chalking them up to bad luck or circumstance. But life doesn't always let you get away with that. When life decides you need to change, it won't let you go until you've faced yourself, raw and unguarded.

It's clear to me now the heartbreaks and losses were life's way of breaking through my defenses, of forcing me to confront truths I didn't want to see. Had I learned the lessons earlier, maybe I wouldn't have had to face such an overwhelming loss. But sometimes, life doesn't leave you with a choice. It forces you into the darkest places so you can grow. Sometimes, it drags you into the darkness because that's the only way to find the light.

There's another part of this story that I've reflected on many times. In our family, the men seem to face the same struggles—your grandfather, my brothers, and me. We all have had failed marriages and money lost. Growing up, I thought I would be different, that I was too good and too cautious to make the same mistakes. But life, in its quiet cruelty, doesn't let anyone escape.

I found myself in situations and made decisions that led me down similar paths. The cycle is real. Was it a generational debt? Was it something we all had to experience to learn a lesson? I'm not sure. The consequences of this cycle—both emotional and financial— reach far beyond what we can see. I watched how it affected your grandfather. He could never escape it, and it took away a part of who he was, draining his spirit.

For me, I've chosen to take this as a lesson to move forward. In the story of my life, this chapter of loss felt inevitable—but not final. Yet, the astrologer's words still echo in my mind. He predicted I would lose money and marry twice. It bothers me, like some cruel joke, but maybe it was part of a greater plan, part of the journey I'm on.

If there's one thing I've learned from all of this, it's this: be careful what you wish for. Be mindful of what you take—whether it's opportunities, trust, or love—and be sure to return it with gratitude. You will cause grief to others—that's inevitable, especially in a competitive world. But causing grief from a place of selfishness or cruelty? That's not how we evolve. Life is meant to move forward, not backward.

It's natural for life to be evolutionary, to progress. And if there's some cosmic bookkeeping for everything you take, you must give back in kind. What you give will come back to you—maybe not right away, but eventually, in some other form.

When I look at you, I feel a deep sense of peace. It reassures me to know that life, despite its chaos, has brought me moments of pure joy—moments like holding you in my lap, feeling the weight of all that is good and true. That, Isha, is balance. And that knowledge brings me comfort.

There's a selfish reason behind any act of giving, Isha. And there should be. We all give because, on some level, we expect something in return. Look at the trees and plants around us—they take carbon from us, and we take oxygen from them. It's a natural exchange. But what stands out is how nature gives. It doesn't just take; it gives more than it ever expects in return. Trees give fruit not just as a gift but as part of their survival. By giving, they continue. And that's the lesson—give not just because it's generous but because it ensures continuity and a sense of abundance. When you live from that abundance, balance becomes as natural as breathing; it's less about receiving and more about knowing you're part of something whole. And when you receive, always be grateful. Life may not return the favor right away or in the ways you expect, but it has a way of balancing things out. Nature, in all its selfishness, still manages to be overwhelmingly generous.

So, where does that leave us? I don't have all the answers, but here's what I believe. Whether or not our lives are preordained, living with an abundance mindset makes sense to me. Giving more than you take, being open to sharing what you have, trusting that life will find its own way to balance things out—that's what I hold on to. Maybe I'm wrong, but it doesn't matter. This belief has brought me peace, and it helps me understand how the world works.

In the end, Isha, I don't know if our lives are written in those ancient leaves or if we're making it up as we go along. Maybe it's a bit of both.

What I do know is that living in fear of scarcity—of not having enough—only limits you. When you open yourself up, when you give freely, life has a way of returning that energy. Maybe that's Karma, as I understand it, or maybe it's just how the universe maintains its balance. Either way, it's a way of living that feels right to me.

So keep moving forward. One step at a time. Trust that balance will find you.

It's not about solving the mystery of fate or free will. It's about asking the right questions—and having the courage to live through the answers. Through that, we create our own balance, one that doesn't need to be written in ancient leaves to be real.

I wonder, Isha, have you ever experienced a moment where loss or failure taught you something valuable—something you couldn't have learned any other way? Do you believe your life is prewritten, or do you feel you shape your own path? And when you stand at a crossroads, uncertain of what lies ahead, how will you trust that life has its own way of finding balance?

With all my love,
Appā

Ready for a story? Here's something I wanted to share with you...

Bangalore, 1980s. Before the city filled with the noise of traffic and endless construction, it breathed easier. In the mornings, the sky still felt wide and quiet, and if you stopped to listen, you could hear the world waking up slowly in the quiet spaces between the trees. It was rightly called the Garden City of India for that reason, and the city was just beautiful.

In one of these quiet streets lived Surya, a middle-aged man, in a house that mirrored the simplicity of his life. It was a small place, a matchbox of a home, with just one living room, one bedroom, a kitchen, and a bathroom. The house stood shoulder to shoulder with others on the street, each one a reflection of the other, as if they were all cut from the same cloth.

Surya's house blended into the rest—a dwelling that stood like all the others. The walls had once held some brightness, but the years had weathered them, the paint fading under the sun's steady glare. The lock on the front door was there more from habit than from any real need.

Inside, they had just enough to get by. The living room served as both a space for their day and, when night came, a place where he'd unfold his cot. The ceiling fan above never spun quite right; its low hum is a sound they learned to live with. The smell of incense mixed with the day's cooking always lingered in the corners of the room, a part of the air they breathed.

The kitchen wasn't much, just a stove and a few pots lined up neatly. His wife moved through it without thought, her bare feet soft against the cool floor. Her sarees, always the same simple cotton, had softened over time, just like her hands—familiar with the rhythm of chopping, stirring, serving, each movement part of her routine.

Their daughters, with their braided hair and bright skirts, filled the house with their constant chatter. They brought the house to life, running from room to room, always laughing, always moving. At night, they spread their mats on the floor next to their mother, curling into the quiet comfort of cotton sheets with no complaints, just sleep.

And sometimes, late in the evening, the breeze would carry in the scent of the Jacaranda tree outside. Its blue flowers had a way of taking him back, though he couldn't explain why. They covered the ground like a memory that stayed with you, even as the world kept moving on. Those flowers always reminded him of the things he hadn't said, the thoughts that drifted in and out of reach.

Every morning started the same way. His wife always packed his lunch—usually rice and sambar, sometimes chapatis and a bit of spiced potatoes and chutney. He'd pack extra, always enough to share with the others at work. Sharing had been second nature to him for as long as he could remember. At work, he'd unpack his lunch and pass it around, offering bits to anyone who sat close by. It wasn't much, but it was a way of letting people know they mattered. Back then, it was just how things were—men were served first, getting the crispiest dosa and the sweetest fruits. He never asked for it, but his wife always set aside the best portions for him, out of habit as much as tradition. Yet, he'd call his daughters over without a second thought, sharing the best bites with them. They didn't need to ask; they knew he'd always offer, including them in life's small treats.

Before heading out, he would often hear her reminding him of the things they needed—the rice that was running low, the overdue water bill, the school fees that would soon be due. These worries never really left him. Even as he cycled down the familiar streets, past old banyan trees and small tea stalls, they sat heavily in his mind.

He worked as a clerk in a government office, his colleagues and his manager living lives much like his own. Middle-class men, all of them, pushing through the same grind, wearing down the same shoes. They were steady men, moving through life without complaint but without much hope for change either. His work wasn't difficult, but it was the kind of job that wore you down slowly. The paperwork never really ended, and the conversations with his colleagues were always the same—school fees, rising prices, and an occasional cricket match. It was a quiet grind; nothing ever changed, but there was a sense of comfort in the routine.

The park near his office was a small patch of green in the middle of the bustling city, shaded by rain trees that had been there longer than he could remember. At lunch, he would walk in the park, buying 15 paise worth of split beans to feed the pigeons. He found peace in the flurry of wings as the birds fought over the scattered beans. It was his moment of quiet, his mind clearing away the paperwork and the endless bills he had to think about. Each day felt the same—work, home, sleep, repeat. Sometimes, he wondered if this was all there was to life and if he would one day grow old watching his daughters take on the same grind. He never wanted that for them. He wanted more, but he didn't know how he could break free from the chains of mediocrity.

Every evening, he walked the last kilometer home from work, pushing his bicycle through the market. This was his time to unwind, to let go of the day's weight. The market bustled with life—vegetable vendors, the smell of fried snacks, and the noise of people moving in every direction. He stopped by familiar stalls, exchanging pleasantries with the vendors he'd known for years—buying tomatoes, green chillis, brinjals, seasonal fruits, and coriander for the next day's meals. It was in these walks, this last stretch of the day, that he felt a brief sense of calm.

It was during one of these walks that he first noticed the lottery stall. He had seen it many times before, but that evening, something caught his eye. The bright colors, the flashing lights, it all seemed to call to him, but he didn't buy a ticket. Not yet. On this particular evening, he overheard two men talking about a new scooter one of their neighbors had bought. A small, harmless detail, but it clung to him. He hadn't bought anything new for the family in years. The fan still rattled above their heads, the paint on the walls had long since faded, and the lock on the front door was more from habit than necessity. Everyone else, it seemed, was moving forward while he stayed in place.

That night, as he lay in bed, his mind wandered to his daughters. They were sleeping peacefully, their small breaths steady in the dark. Would they be trapped in the same cycle he was—getting by but never really getting ahead? What was he leaving behind for them? Would they one day look back at their lives and wonder why he hadn't given them more? Would they grow up with dreams unfulfilled, the way he had been? These thoughts gnawed at him, and for the first time, the quiet hope of winning the lottery became more than just a fleeting idea. Maybe he could change something for them, offer them more than just the comfort of their small home.

A few days later, he saw a friend buying a ticket at the stall. They exchanged pleasantries, and the friend explained how he played the last three numbers and had won a few times. "It's not much," his friend said, "but it's something." That evening, for the first time, he bought a ticket. Five rupees. He felt the familiar weight of the 5 rupees in his hand as he passed it to the lottery vendor. It could have bought his daughters a few sweets or a handful of vegetables for dinner, but today, it was for something else—a fleeting hope of a better tomorrow.

He asked for the same numbers his friend had chosen. He didn't expect much, but the small flicker of hope stayed with him. As he handed over the money, he felt a small flutter of hope, something he hadn't allowed himself to feel in a long time. He took the ticket home and placed it carefully under his pillow as if guarding a secret. All night, he thought about what might happen if he won, the possibilities stirring in his mind.

The next day, when the results came in, he was surprised to find he had won fifteen rupees. It wasn't a lot, but it lit a spark. He found his friend and told him the good news. His friend showed him a small notebook he kept, tracking the numbers, the wins, the losses. "You see, there's a pattern to it," his friend said, tapping the notepad. "One day, I'm going to crack the code, retire, and take my family to Goa." At home that night, he couldn't sleep well. He kept thinking about the win that night, and he couldn't wait to go buy another one the next day.

That first win was enough to spark a quiet obsession. He started buying tickets more regularly, tracking numbers, and following his friend's advice. He would spend his evenings scribbling down figures, trying to piece together the puzzle. There had to be a pattern, a rhythm hidden in the chaos of numbers. If he could just figure it out, it would all make sense. He could win. He could break free. Every ticket he bought felt like one step closer to unlocking the answer.

It started with small amounts—five rupees here, ten there. The wins weren't much, but they were enough to keep him up at night, going over numbers, convinced he was getting closer to something. He didn't give it much thought at first. The tickets were tucked away in a drawer, out of sight, but they lingered in his mind more than he realized.

At work, it began to seep into his routine. His desk, once organized, now had bits of paper with numbers scribbled on them and calculations scattered between the files. He kept it hidden from his manager, but the urge to figure it out followed him, pressing in when he least expected it. He began noticing patterns, sure that if he kept at it, the numbers would eventually give him what he was searching for. He believed that the next ticket would be the one to change everything.

It wasn't just the lottery anymore. Soon, everything started to feel connected—cricket scores, football matches, even the casual bets with friends over tea. "There's a pattern here," he'd say, tossing out his theories as if they were casual, though deep down, he was beginning to believe there was a code waiting to be solved. He wasn't sure when the shift had happened, but by then, there was no going back. He was convinced that the answer was out there— he just had to keep searching.

At first, it seemed harmless, a way to fill the time. But as the days passed, the numbers started following him everywhere—into the quiet of his home, into the stillness of the night when everyone else was asleep. The small wins kept him going, feeding something inside him and pushing him to keep trying. His colleagues noticed the change. They started asking him for advice, and it felt good to be the one with the answers, even if those answers were nothing more than guesses.

The deeper he went, the less it was about money. It became about finding the answer, about figuring out the puzzle that seemed just out of reach. His notebook, once a place for random notes, filled up with rows of numbers, each one feeling like a piece of a larger picture that he was desperate to see.

At home, his wife didn't say anything, but she knew something was different. She saw it in the way his eyes drifted, even when he was sitting right there with them. The space between them wasn't loud, but it was there. She didn't push, maybe waiting for him to come back to where he used to be.

But he didn't. Not yet.

The sun had started to dip when he lay down for a moment, hoping the weight on his chest would ease. Sleep came reluctantly, tugging him under, and when it did, it brought no comfort. He found himself in a field, a pot of gold sitting just beyond his reach, shimmering against the dirt. He wanted to run to it, to grab hold, but his feet sank deeper into the earth with every step. The harder he tried, the more the ground swallowed him up. The gold stayed where it was, mocking him as he sank further.

He woke with a start, his body stiff, the dream still clinging to him. The sound of his daughters' laughter filled the room, pulling him back. They ran to him, climbing onto his lap, their little fingers brushing against his face. "Appā, you had a bad dream?" one asked, giggling, her voice soft. He pulled her close, her warmth grounding him, but the guilt gnawed at him.

"Appā, we're hungry," his younger daughter said, her small hands tugging at his shirt. He held them both tighter for a moment, then stood up slowly, leading them toward the kitchen. He knew what he would find there, but the reality of it hit him harder than he had expected.

The cupboard door creaked as he opened it, and his chest tightened. A small glass of rice, a few lentils—that was it. The vegetables had given up days ago, their wilted remains already tossed out.

He wondered how his wife had managed at all with so little in the house. She must have trusted that he had something left, a few bills tucked away, enough to stretch until she returned. The thought sat heavy in his stomach. He felt bad—worse than bad. The guilt of his new habit gnawed at him.

She had believed he would manage. That there was enough. That he wouldn't let things slip. And yet, here he was.

He stood there, staring at the emptiness, the reality of his choices hanging over him like a dark cloud. His daughters stood by the door, their innocent faces waiting for him to cook them dinner. "Let's go for a walk, get ready" he said, his voice even though inside, he was crumbling. The girls jumped up in joy and got ready quickly. They very rarely went to the market with their father, and they knew their father always bought them sweets, unlike their mother, who was a bit more stringent.

As they left the house, he didn't know how he would manage. But he hoped. Hope was all he had left.

They walked through the market, his daughters skipping beside him, their hands warm in his. The usual sounds—the calls of the vegetable vendors, the clatter of pots, the sizzle of frying snacks— felt distant today, as if he was moving through a haze. The smells that once filled him with comfort now only reminded him of what he couldn't provide.

As they passed the lottery stall, he stopped, something in him hesitating. He had passed it many times before, but today, it seemed to pull him in. The flashing lights, the spot lottery sign— they were the same as always. He felt the last five rupees in his pocket. His daughters tugged at his hands, unaware of the quiet storm inside him.

The right thing would be to buy some groceries, take them home, and make something as their mother would have done. But the temptation of a spot win that evening was too strong. Maybe it was his time; it had to be tonight; I have my daughters with me this time, he thought. Maybe today.

His chest tightened as he handed it over, as if he were giving away more than just money.

Without another word, he handed over the five rupees.

His daughters, oblivious to the gravity of the moment, looked around at the bustling market, their small hands clinging to his, trusting that their father had everything under control. As they clung to his hands, their small fingers warm and trusting, he felt the weight of their innocence pressing down on him. They looked up at him with wide, expectant eyes, and he couldn't bear the thought of them knowing the truth—that the man they looked to for everything had gambled away their security for a fleeting dream.

The result came, and it was a loss. He stared at the ticket in disbelief, his mind racing with the reality of their situation. There was no money left and nothing to bring home for dinner. He wanted to cry, to tell his daughters the truth that they would have to go home empty-handed, but the words wouldn't come. As they walked through the market, his mind was elsewhere. His pockets were nearly empty, and the thought of what awaited him at home—a kitchen with barely half a glass of rice—hung over him like a cloud.

Just as he was about to admit defeat, a sweet corn vendor passed by. His daughters, their eyes wide with excitement, tugged at his hand. "Appā, can we have one?"

Before he could respond, the vendor, an old friend, smiled and handed them two pieces of sweet corn, roasted and steaming. "For you, my little girls," the vendor said, clapping him on the back. "It's on the house today."

Relief washed over him, but it wasn't enough to push away the guilt. As they moved through the market, he was about to explain to the girls that they would have to go home empty-handed. He felt like crying, the weight of it all crashing down on him. But just then, a familiar voice called out. The vegetable vendor, an older woman who had known him for years, walked over and rubbed his daughters' heads. She handed them some fresh vegetables to the daughters, smiling warmly. "Take these home and give it to your mother," she said, refusing his money. "Your father comes to me every day, but he never told me about these little darlings."

Tears welled up in his eyes, but he thanked her and moved on, his heart heavy but slightly lifted by the kindness. As they passed the oil merchant and the sweet seller, his daughter noticed a man in a lungi running towards them. He looked back, seeing their fear, but it was only the shop assistant from the provision store running toward them with a bag of rice in his hands.

"Aiya wanted you to have this," the assistant said, out of breath. "He overcharged you last time by accident and felt bad about it. He just remembered it when he saw you now." The assistant then handed him the bag of rice and said, "Take this, please; forgive us."

The shopkeeper, busy behind his counter, waved in apology from a distance. The kindness of these familiar faces in the market chipped away at the weight pressing on his heart. He could no longer hold back his tears, holding the bag in one hand, carrying one daughter in the other, with his other daughter clinging to his shirt. He didn't care who saw him crying; he needed it.

As they walked home, the girls munching on their corn, he felt something shift inside him. The numbers, the tickets—they had taken more than just his money. They had robbed him of his peace, his time, and the moments he used to find joy in the small things. And for what? A dream that was never meant to be.

He thought back to the many evenings spent hunched over his notes, scribbling down combinations, chasing patterns. How many times had he missed his daughters' laughter, the warmth of their company, because his mind was elsewhere, lost in numbers that never gave him what he hoped for? The real cost wasn't the money—it was the time that slipped through his fingers, the time he would never get back.

He reached into his pocket without thinking, his fingers brushing against the crumpled lottery tickets. He hadn't meant to pull them out, but there they were, a reminder of everything that had consumed him. Without hesitation, he tore the tickets in half and threw them into the nearest bin. He didn't need them anymore.

His daughters' laughter echoed in the small house when they finally returned home, and for the first time in months, he didn't feel that tight knot in his chest. There was nothing weighing on him anymore—just the sound of them, and that felt right. He watched them—those bright eyes, the way they smiled so easily— and it hit him: he'd had enough all along. More than enough.

That evening, he went into the kitchen and made a meal. Nothing fancy, but it wasn't about the food, not really. It was the way the room felt as he chopped vegetables, stirred the pot, and listened to the quiet hum of the house. They had never gone without, not really. Somehow, even when it felt like there was nothing, there had always been enough to feed them, enough to keep them going.

For months, he had chased after something more, convinced that a windfall would fix everything. But now, as he stood in the kitchen, watching his daughters eat the meal he had prepared, it all seemed so clear. It wasn't more money he needed. It was never about the money.

The truth, he realized, was that he had been afraid. Afraid that he wasn't enough for his family, that one day his daughters would grow up and look back at a life that felt too small. Afraid that he would never escape the quiet grind of mediocrity that had become his world.

Later, when his wife came back, tired from being with her mother, the girls wrapped themselves around her, giggling. He watched them, standing there with her, and for the first time in what felt like forever, the house felt full in a way that money couldn't buy. He realized then that it wasn't about winning; it never had been. It was about the people in his life, the ones who made sure they were always okay, even when it didn't seem like it.

That night, as his daughters slept soundly on the mats, he lay awake, listening to their breathing, realizing something he should have seen all along. They had never gone hungry—not once. Somehow, even when it felt like the cupboards were bare, life had a way of filling the gaps, whether it was a neighbor's generosity or just enough money to buy a little rice.

It wasn't the lottery that mattered, not the one he had been chasing. The real thing, the real win, was the way life had kept giving, even when he hadn't noticed. He didn't need to hit the jackpot to see that.

He smiled to himself in the dark, a small, quiet smile. He had already won.

As he lay awake that night, listening to the soft breathing of his daughters, the events of the past few months finally began to settle in his mind. All this time, he had been waiting for something bigger—a jackpot, a sudden windfall. But life had never stopped giving. It had come in small, quiet ways: the way his wife stretched their meals, the way neighbors filled the gaps when things ran low, and the laughter of his daughters.

He realized now that he hadn't needed the big win. He had been searching for something more when what he needed was already here—within the simple, everyday moments that had always kept them afloat.

There had always been enough. And in that realization, for the first time, he felt like he could breathe.

Letting Go, Holding On

Part 1: The Weight of Possessions

Isha,

We have been blessed with a good life. I say "blessed" not in a religious sense, but because gratitude settles quietly in me when I think of where we are.

You are five as I write this, and as I see you grow up, I also see you very attached to the things around you, and it doesn't come easy for you to share. It's natural at your age, this fierce desire to hold on to everything, to claim it as yours. There are three boxes of toys and Legos that you've told me not to give away to the Salvation Army because you're not ready to let go of them, along with a jacket you don't wear anymore and pairs of shoes that are three sizes too small still tucked away in the cabinet. Perhaps it's just a phase of childhood, but I hope as you grow, you'll start to understand the joy and freedom that comes with letting go. There's a lightness in passing things on, knowing someone else might cherish them.

It's the same reason I stick to simple things—even my clothes. You once asked me, 'Why do you always wear dark T-shirts?' I smiled and said, 'I like it that way.' But it's more than that. Simplifying my choices, even in something as small as what I wear, gives me room to focus on what truly matters. It's not about deprivation— it's about clarity. That's the essence of letting go: to strip away the unnecessary distractions and make room for what truly adds meaning to your life.

Your mother and I haven't always been overly particular about keeping our doors locked all the time. We're in a good neighborhood, and we felt secure. But that's changed for me in the last six months. You see, a friend from Bangalore recently developed a passion for collecting memorabilia—watches, antiques, little treasures that hold stories. He ordered seven packages of these things and had them delivered to our home for safekeeping until Christmas when he planned to visit and pick them up.

Since those packages arrived, my nights have changed. Every sound wakes me. Every flicker of the security light holds my breath hostage. I check the locks once, then again. Sleep feels lighter, like I'm waiting for something to happen. It's like I've become the sage from an old Indian story my father once told me.

The story goes like this: A sage on a pilgrimage travels across the country with a few students. At night, they eat whatever people have offered them along the way. One day, a dejected king crosses their path, seeking advice. The sage, wise as he is, offers some wisdom that transforms the king's thinking. Grateful, the king insists on rewarding the sage with 100 gold coins. At first, the sage resists, but eventually, he accepts the gift.

That's when everything changes. With the gold in his possession, the sage becomes anxious, guarding the coins as if his life depended on them. He starts keeping an eye out for robbers, grows suspicious of his own students, and hardly sleeps at night. One night, the inevitable happens: a group of robbers attacks. The sage fights back with all his might, only to be defeated and left on his knees.

The robbers, expecting great treasure, find the bag contains nothing but annas—coins barely worth anything. Confused, they laugh and leave. The sage, shaken and humiliated, learns that one of his students had secretly thrown the gold into a well weeks ago.

For months, the sage had been guarding a worthless bag with his life.

Lately, I've felt like that sage—guarding treasures that aren't mine, losing peace over things that don't belong to me. It's a reminder: sometimes, it's not the possessions themselves, but the weight we give them, that takes something from us. In today's world, it might not be a bag of coins, but the anxiety over things—whether it's the fear of losing a job, a house, or even the data on our phones—can trap us just as tightly. We guard them, letting their weight dictate our lives, forgetting that real treasures are far simpler.

But then there are moments that remind me of what truly matters. Just a few mornings ago, I sat on the balcony with a cup of tea, doing absolutely nothing. I looked around and felt such deep appreciation for where we live. Up here, away from the noise and crowds, surrounded by lush greenery, there's a stillness that seeps into you.

This house—it feels like a part of me now. Isha, this is a place where I find it easy to write and meditate. The steep driveway leading up the hill, the towering trees—almost 18 of them (well, 17 now since I cut one down last summer)—everything about this place feels grounding. These trees have been here longer than I have, and many will outlast me. They're silent witnesses to the passing of time, indifferent to our comings and goings.

In that stillness, it struck me—I don't own this place. I never did. I'm just passing through, a guest in this space, as temporary as the shadows that shift across the walls. The trees, the plants—they've accepted me into their midst, and we coexist. Ownership is an illusion, Isha. When we see life this way, we realize that nothing is really ours—it's all borrowed. It sounds philosophical, but it's also freeing. When you see life this way, ownership loses its weight.

We're all just passing through, aren't we? And for now, I get to sit on this balcony and call it home.

I've shared this with you before, but growing up, we had very little. My family didn't own a place in Bangalore until I was in my twenties. Before that, we lived in a small, cramped unit—one living space where my father and I shared the floor, and my mother and sisters shared the bedroom. There was no privacy, no extra space, and very few possessions. But we made it work. We had what we needed, and maybe that's what taught me to appreciate the things we did have.

Part 2: The Mark of Loss

Loss has a strange way of leaving its mark. It doesn't matter if it's a bicycle, a notebook, or an entire life you've built over decades— each loss teaches you something different. It doesn't just take away; it leaves a shadow, shaping how you see the world and what you choose to hold on to. I want to tell you a story about loss—one that shaped me deeply.

One of the few things my father owned and loved was his bicycle. It wasn't fancy, but it was his, and it served him well. Most of my childhood memories seem tied to that bike. I never learned to ride on it, but it was always there, part of our daily lives. Then, one day, a distant relative came to stay with us for a month. He was polite and helpful, a comforting presence in our small household. He ran errands, walked us to school, and even assisted my mother with shopping. My father liked him so much that he recommended him for a job.

But one morning, as I was getting ready for school, this relative borrowed the bike for an errand. "Just a quick ride," he said. He never came back. That day, we walked to school, and I remember asking my mother repeatedly, "Has the bike come back yet? Has he come back yet?" Her answer stayed the same: no.

The loss of that bicycle struck us all. We didn't have much, and this wasn't just a bike—it was something my father cherished. Its absence lingered. He eventually bought another bike, this time with a motor. But the loss had changed him. He kept this new bike inside the house, in the tiny living space we shared with six people because he couldn't trust anyone with it anymore.

Watching my father guard his new bike, I saw how fear of loss can distort the joy of having something we value. I wasn't immune to that fear myself. For a long time, I was careful—sometimes overly so—when it came to the things I owned. But time has shaped me, Isha. Now, I no longer hoard. Instead, I cherish what I have. I am glad that my father's reaction to that loss didn't shape my own views on possessions. I have learned that joy comes not from clinging but from sharing—especially with those I love. If someone in the family enjoys something I have, it brings me more happiness than owning it ever could.

Still, Isha, loss leaves its mark. When I was 34, I lost almost everything for the first time. Then again, at 44, I experienced another wave of loss—less dramatic but no less painful. It was as if life itself worked on a ten-year cycle, stripping me bare to remind me of what truly mattered. The first time, I still had hope, but the second time was different. It felt heavier, more permanent. I remember lying in bed, unable to see a way forward. That's when these letters began.

Loss is cruel like that. It strips you down, leaving you raw and exposed, forcing you to decide what you'll rebuild and what you'll leave behind. For me, the hardest losses weren't the material ones—they were the irreplaceable pieces of memory and meaning.

Take my writing, for example. Over the years, I've written notebooks filled with thoughts, observations, and moments I wanted to remember. I've lost some of them to moves, some to carelessness, and some to circumstances I couldn't control. Each time, it stings. When I try to recreate what I've lost, I find that it's impossible. I'm not the same person who wrote those words. I can't be the 21-year-old nervous about his first flight or the man sitting by his dying father, capturing his last words. Those moments are gone, and with them, the person I was.

There's one notebook I lost that haunts me still. It was a travel journal I kept after your grandfather passed away. I'd written about my time in Tamil Nadu—small towns, temples, fleeting encounters with strangers. That notebook, along with my personal laptop and camera, was left behind when I walked out of my first marriage. I didn't think clearly that night, and the notebook stayed behind with the rest of my life at the time. In the chaos of that night, I didn't think clearly. For months, I tried to recreate it, but the journal wasn't just words on paper. It was a snapshot of a moment in time—a moment I can't go back to.

Some things, like notebooks and photos, are irreplaceable. Over the years, I've learned to protect the things that matter most to me. Today, with everything stored in the cloud, I don't worry as much about losing pictures. But if the world ever goes dark, I hope you keep a few physical photos with you. They're not just keepsakes; they're anchors, holding entire lifetimes within their edges.

There's another category of possessions that's equally precious: keepsakes. I still have your grandfather's shirt and watch. These aren't just objects—they're threads connecting me to a man who shaped so much of who I am. They carry his presence, his strength, and even his flaws. If you ever find yourself in a position to save just one thing from a fire or flood, let it be something that holds meaning—not monetary value.

But here's the paradox of loss: while it teaches you to hold on to what matters, it also teaches you to let go. I've walked out of houses with nothing but a laundry basket holding all my belongings. I've stood in empty rooms and felt both exposed and free. There's a strange liberation in starting over—a lightness that comes with shedding the weight of who you were.

If you ever find yourself in that position, Isha—starting over—don't be afraid. Strip down to the basics. Let go of everything you don't need, and then add back only the things that truly serve you. Everything else is just noise, cluttering your space and your mind.

In the end, loss isn't about what's taken away—it's about what you choose to rebuild. It's a crucible, Isha, forging strength from sorrow. And Isha, you are strong enough to rebuild anything.

Part 3: The Meaning of Things

There's a strange relationship we have with the things we own. They're just objects, yet they hold so much meaning—sometimes more than we realize. I've spent a lifetime learning how to navigate this relationship, and as I reflect, I see how it has shaped me.

When I was younger, we didn't own much. Our home was a single living space where six of us lived, worked, and slept. Yet, somehow, it didn't feel small. It was just life as we knew it. It was our world, one defined not by space but by the people within it. I didn't envy the kids with bigger houses or more toys because I didn't have the concept of "more" back then. What we had felt enough, and in hindsight, those moments were among the richest of my life.

But there's something you should know about things: they can both enrich your life and weigh you down. As a child, I watched my father learn this the hard way. After losing his bicycle, he became so protective of his possessions that he kept his new motorbike inside our already cramped home. It was his way of safeguarding something he valued, but it also showed me how fear can distort our relationship with the things we own.

When I moved out on my own, I swung to the opposite extreme. A friend once joked that I "lived like a monk" because my apartment was so sparsely furnished. And he wasn't wrong—there was a couch, a bed, a bedside table, and a juicer. That was it. But I never felt like I was missing anything. My life was full in other ways—in experiences, connections, and the work I was doing.

Over time, though, I realized it wasn't about having nothing or having everything—it was about balance. The things we choose to keep should serve us, not define us. They should bring joy, not clutter. That's why, when your mother gets into one of her Marie Kondo moods and starts clearing out the house, I don't argue. Sometimes, you don't realize how much space you've been holding for things you don't even need.

But, Isha, it's also okay to love the things you own. I would be lying if I said I wasn't attached to certain possessions. I love the richness they bring to life—good wine, a beautifully crafted meal, a well-worn jacket, or an adventure that costs more than it probably should. What's the point of a good life if you don't enjoy it? But the key is to love them without letting them own you. It's about knowing what to hold on to and what to let go of.

Isha, there was a day when I nearly gave everything away—every piece of clothing, every object, every attachment. I imagined walking into an empty house, my bare feet against the cold floor, ready to rebuild my life from scratch. I didn't do it, but the thought alone felt like freedom. It reminded me that who I am isn't defined by the things I own but by the life I live.

If you ever find yourself in a place where you need to start over, I hope you'll embrace it. Strip down to the basics. Hold on only to what matters—what truly brings you joy or meaning. Let everything else fall away. Life is too short to be weighed down by things that don't serve you.

But there are exceptions. Some things are worth protecting. For me, it's my notebooks, my father's shirt, and his watch. These aren't just objects—they're pieces of my story. They connect me to moments, to people, and to a past that has shaped me. Losing those would be like losing a part of myself.

Even in today's world, where everything is stored in the cloud, I still believe in keeping a few physical photos. They ground you in a way that no digital file ever can. These little things—objects, photos, keepsakes—they're not just things. They're anchors in the ever-changing tides of life. They remind us of where we come from and who we are.

Isha, my hope for you is this: find your own balance. Don't let the fear of loss rule you, but don't dismiss the value they can bring either. Surround yourself with what matters—whether it's people, objects, or experiences—and let the rest fall away.

Because at its core, life isn't about what you own—it's about what you hold in your heart. Possessions will come and go, but those intangible things—the essence of who you are—can never be taken away.

So, when life takes something away, don't despair. When you choose to let go, don't fear the emptiness. Both are invitations to grow, to create space for new possibilities.

Everything we own is temporary, Isha. Even our memories fade, even the things we cherish will, at some point, no longer be in our hands. But what remains is what we choose to carry—not in our arms, but in our hearts.

In the end, you are not defined by the things you own or lose. You are defined by what you build, the love you give, the moments you create. That is the only real possession that stays with you.

I'll leave you with this:

What will you choose to carry, and what will you let go? Why does it matter to you? Are you keeping it because it brings you joy or because you're afraid to let go? And when the time comes to make space for something new, how will you decide what truly belongs in your life?

Because in answering that, you won't just find clarity—you'll find yourself.

Yours, Appā.

Living With the Shadow

There was a time when the world lost its color. I didn't just feel lost; I felt erased. I slipped into a void, no longer sure of who I was. Everything that once gave my life meaning faded. What I had built—my sense of self, my relationships, my dreams—began to fall apart.

Each day, I drifted further away from the person I once knew. I couldn't even recognize myself. The mirror showed a stranger: a gaunt face, hollow eyes, a shell of the person I used to be. My reflection became a painful reminder of how far I had fallen, how much of myself I had lost to the darkness.

The physical toll was undeniable. I lost 12 kilos in a matter of months, though I couldn't tell you exactly when or how. Food had no taste, and I barely had the energy to get through each day. Sleep felt impossible, haunted by nightmares every time I closed my eyes. Each day was a battle against my own mind, filled with regret and thoughts I couldn't escape.

In the depths of this darkness, I stumbled into parts of myself that were unrecognizable. I discovered parts of myself I didn't even know existed. It was a place beyond pain, where physical suffering became almost irrelevant. The darkness consumed everything, dragging me through horrors that felt too real to be nightmares. I wasn't living anymore—I was just surviving, a shadow of who I had been.

This wasn't just sadness. It was a darkness that seeped into every part of me, poisoning every thought, every moment. I reached the point where the idea of disappearing seemed merciful—not just for me, but for everyone around me.

Every interaction felt like a struggle. Words, once a refuge, felt sharp and alien. Small talk seemed pointless, each word only highlighting the distance between my world and theirs. I could barely make eye contact, afraid they'd glimpse the emptiness inside me. Friends and family tried to offer comfort, but their words were like faint echoes in a hollow room—brief, meaningless, never truly reaching me. The happiness in other people's lives felt like a cruel reminder of what I had lost, a painful contrast to the void I carried. I started isolating myself, pushing away those who cared, convinced that no one could understand the depth of my despair.

Just getting through the day became a chore. The only reason to get out of bed was to power up the laptop, shuffle through spreadsheets, and respond to work emails—the bare minimum to keep the wheels turning.

Days and nights blurred into one long, endless loop of torment. The sameness of it all dulled even the sharp edges of pain. Mornings brought no relief, just a short pause before the cycle started again. The sunlight outside felt mocking, its warmth clashing painfully with the cold emptiness I felt inside.

Evenings were the hardest. The quiet of my home only made the chaos in my mind louder. I would sit for hours, staring blankly, lost in a fog of despair. Regret and guilt circled around me like a storm I couldn't escape, wearing me down with every passing moment.

But nights were the worst. As darkness fell outside, it mirrored the darkness within me. I'd lie in bed, staring at the ceiling, crushed by the weight of my thoughts. It felt like drowning in a bottomless sea, every breath a struggle against an invisible tide. Nightmares blended with reality, and I'd see shadows moving, hear whispers that weren't there, and feel a cold that seeped deep into my bones.

Yet, in a strange way, the nights were also a little better. At night, I didn't have to perform. I didn't have to explain or pretend. Alone with my thoughts, I could be myself without the pressure to fake being okay around family. It was a cold comfort, but at least it felt real.

I started drinking more. People who haven't crossed the line into that level of pain might call it a coping mechanism, but it was more than that. It became my companion. The routine of it—the decision to drink, the purchase, the smell, the color, the pour, the first sip, the act itself—became a ritual that brought me comfort. The bottle was steady in a way I wasn't, predictable in a way life no longer felt. It wasn't about escaping reality; it was about finding solace in the chaos. It was the one thing in my life that asked for nothing and offered silence in return. I'm not glorifying it, but in that phase of my life, it was the one thing that made sense.

And then, I began to write. The pen didn't judge. The page didn't demand answers. I was myself—free from the weight of morality, correctness, or any structured writing rules. In that rawness, I found my voice. For the first time after a very long time, my writing felt raw and honest, a true reflection of who I was.

Glass empty like my soul
Words slur,
Thoughts stumble
Who am I in this haze?
Just a shadow, fading
Tick tock of the clock
Mocking each wasted moment
Alone in this room
Darkness, my only friend

The Abyss

Last night, restless,
I pondered a place for my soul,
Where rivers gulp down their thirst,
And bread isn't as hard as the road I'm on.
I found one damn truth,
Strong as the drink in my hand,
That nobody,
Absolutely nobody,
Makes it alone in this wasteland.

You may wonder what this darkness I speak of truly looks like, what it really means. It's a question I asked myself before settling on the term 'darkness' to describe it. Sometimes, a thought becomes so heavy that it dominates your mind, leaving no space for anything else. It becomes the only thing that matters, building fear with every passing moment. Any attempt to avoid it only makes that fear grow. I stopped smiling, stopped interacting, stopped eating. And when I didn't stop, when I pushed through daily life, my mind was consumed by it. It ruled me.

The darkness wasn't just around me; it lived within me. It was a silence that grew louder with every passing moment, a loneliness that refused to leave. Every day felt like trudging through thick mud, each step an immense effort. While the world continued to turn, I was stuck, trapped in a personal hell of my own making. The vibrant, chaotic energy of life felt distant—something I could see but no longer touch. I felt completely disconnected from reality as if I were floating in a void. Even the simplest tasks became monumental, and each morning brought a crushing sense of dread, knowing I had to survive another 24 hours in this state.

There was no escaping it. No light at the end of the tunnel—only darkness. And this darkness crept into every part of my life. It stole my friendships, caused my wife to look at me with disappointment, and eroded any respect I had for myself. Slowly, it convinced me that I was a failure. I couldn't stop thinking about it, distancing myself from everything just to give that thought space to grow. And it did grow—one dark thought spiraling into another, weaving a web of self-doubt and hopelessness. I began to fall deeper into it.

In every corner of that labyrinth, nightmares lurked. The line between reality and imagination blurred, trapping me in an unending loop of fear and despair. Nights were the worst—filled with haunting visions, restless tossing and turning. I'd wake up drenched in sweat, my heart pounding, the remnants of nightmares clinging to my mind like a fog I couldn't shake.

The darkness came in shades. Some days, it was so thick and suffocating that its arrival alone brought memories of what it meant to be consumed by it, and I desperately searched for ways to avoid it. These were the days when there was no lifeline long enough to keep me afloat. The darkness was an old, familiar enemy—a constant reminder of battles fought and lost time and time again.

On other days, the darkness was more of a dull, pervasive gloom that seeped into everything. It wasn't as intense but just as suffocating. It drained the color from my world, leaving everything gray and lifeless. On those days, I moved through life like a ghost— unseen, untouched. I went through the motions, but my heart wasn't in it. The darkness lingered like a shadow, always whispering that this was my new reality and there was no way out.

My body ached with a fatigue no amount of sleep could fix, a weariness that settled deep into my bones. The simplest tasks felt monumental, a climb I couldn't muster the strength for. I would often catch myself staring into nothingness, too drained to move or think. It felt like my very essence was being sapped, leaving only an empty shell behind.

Drinking became a ritual, more of a companion than a mere coping mechanism. The hours spent with a drink in hand weren't unbearable—they were a brief respite from the constant storm raging inside me. It wasn't about the escape but the familiarity. The routine of it, as said before, became a ritual that brought me comfort. The bottle was steady in a way I wasn't, predictable in a way life no longer felt. It didn't fix the darkness, but it dulled the sharp edges and gave me a place to rest. It was silent support, free of judgment, a time when I could sit alone with my thoughts without the pressure of explaining myself or meeting anyone's expectations.

Even drinking carried a certain sadness with it—a reminder of the solitude that had come to define me. I'd sit on the balcony or lie in bed, glass in hand, watching the world go by. The people outside felt so distant, their lives moving on as mine stood still. They laughed, they chatted, and they had a purpose while I remained trapped in a web of my own making. The drink became a symbol of my isolation, a quiet companion in the quiet, and a marker of how far I'd fallen.

In those quiet moments of solitude, I would often find myself reflecting on the past—on the choices I made and the paths I didn't take. Regret clung to me, a constant voice in my head, reminding me of every mistake, every missed opportunity. It was relentless, never giving me a moment's peace. I'd replay conversations and interactions over and over, dissecting every word, every gesture, convinced that somehow I had failed in ways I couldn't undo.

The darkness was absolute, unyielding. There was no navigating it, no learning to live alongside it. It was an all-consuming force that left no space for hope or escape. Every day, I confronted this reality—a reality I feared might consume me entirely.

Can't sleep, can't think straight
Memories haunt,
Regrets linger
Bottles line up,
Soldiers in my war against myself,
Against the quiet
City sleeps
While I drown in a sea of what-ifs and maybes
Loneliness wraps around me tight as a noose.

Crisis Points

One night, I took Milo for a walk by the bay, not far from your grandparents' home in Waverton. The water was dark and cold, mirroring how I felt inside. I thought about stepping in, letting the water take me. You, Isha. You were always in my mind. And the letters—I had been writing for you, tracing pieces of myself onto a page, hoping they would outlast me. Those letters became my reason to keep going. They were my way of reaching out to you. And there was Milo, standing beside me, looking into my eyes.

There were many times when the darkness felt overwhelming. Each time, I found myself at a crossroads. One path led to nothing, the other to more pain. The darkness kept whispering that ending it all was the only way out. But something always stopped me— whether it was the thought of your smile or the feeling of a pen in my hand as I wrote to you.

One night, while everyone was asleep, I sat by the window. The house was silent. I pressed my forehead against the cold glass, staring at the city lights through my tears. I couldn't breathe. I felt so alone like I was drowning. But thinking of you kept me afloat. I clung to that thought with everything I had.

Another bad day came at work. Everything looked normal, but inside, I was unraveling. I had to retreat to the bathroom to calm myself down. My heart was racing, and I could barely breathe. I wanted to disappear. Then, my boss said something kind. It wasn't much, but it was enough to get me through that day.

The intensity of the darkness shifted, too. Some days, it was heavy, making it hard to move or think. On other days, it was sharp and painful. Those were the days when giving up felt like it might be a relief.

Sometimes, I'd catch a glimpse of clarity. These moments didn't last long, but they reminded me that the darkness wasn't everything. There were small cracks where the light found its way in.

Writing these letters to you was difficult, but it also helped. It forced me to confront my darkest thoughts. Each letter helped me untangle the chaos in my mind. It gave me a reason to keep fighting, even when I felt like I couldn't continue.

In the end, it was the little things that kept me going—thinking of your smile, remembering an act of kindness, writing these letters. These small moments kept me grounded, tethered to the world. They gave me the strength to keep fighting, even when the darkness felt overwhelming.

I'm still unsure if the darkness will ever truly disappear. It feels like a part of me now, like a shadow that follows wherever I go. The good moments don't last long—they're fragile and fleeting.

Darkness

Sometimes, the darkness felt like a physical weight pressing down on my chest, making it hard to breathe. One day at work, everything seemed normal at first. Then suddenly, the world felt wrong. The lights were too bright, and people's voices too loud. I felt exposed like I had no skin.

I had to escape to the bathroom again. I seemed to rush to the bathroom—the cubicle in the bathroom, narrow and confined, felt safe. I locked myself in and sat on the floor, struggling to remember how to breathe. The cold tiles helped a little. I felt so alone, even though the building was full of people. I just wanted to disappear.

But then, I thought of you. Your laugh, your smile. Your mother's tears. And Milo. It was like grabbing onto a rope in the middle of a storm. That thought helped me stand up, wash my face, and return to my desk. It helped me keep going.

The bad times kept returning. Some days, the darkness was just there, making everything feel dull and gray. Other days, it was so intense that it clouded my mind, making it impossible to think straight. Not knowing which version of the darkness I'd face each day made it harder.

I remember one night when I couldn't sleep. The house was so quiet. The ticking clock was a reminder of how alone I felt. I wandered from room to room, my thoughts getting darker. The walls seemed to close in on me. I wanted to run, but there was nowhere to go—the darkness wasn't a place; it was inside me.

Writing to you helped during these times. The sound of the pen and the words forming on the page made the fear feel less overwhelming. Each letter reflected my struggle. Sometimes, writing was painful because it forced me to face things I wanted to forget. But it also helped release the weight of those feelings.

Isha, this darkness isn't something I can defeat. It's part of me now, like my heartbeat. I'm not trying to get rid of it anymore; just learning to live with it. Some days, that means just getting out of bed. On other days, it's finding small moments of light amidst the chaos.

Coping With It

When things were at their worst, I found something that helped: writing. The first time I tried to put my feelings into words, it seemed impossible. But as I began, something shifted. Each word I wrote felt like a small victory against the darkness.

I wrote mostly at night when I couldn't sleep. The sound of the pen on paper was often the only noise in the quiet house. The soft glow of my desk lamp kept the darkness at bay, if only for a little while.

Some days, the words flowed easily, and my hand struggled to keep up with my thoughts. On other days, even writing a single line felt like a battle. The paper often bore the weight of my struggle—sometimes stained with tears, other times crumpled in frustration.

Writing helped me see what was happening in my mind. I started noticing patterns in my thoughts, understanding what triggered me and what kept coming back. It didn't solve everything, but it gave me a glimpse of clarity.

Occasionally, in the middle of writing, something about myself would click. These moments didn't last long, but they were significant. They reminded me that my mind still worked, even in the darkest of times.

Writing forced me to confront the things I feared—my regrets, my flaws, all the parts of myself I didn't want to face. It was incredibly hard, like looking at a wound you'd rather ignore.

But in facing those fears, I found a kind of strength. My words became a way to speak up, even when I felt like giving up. At first, this voice was barely a whisper, but with each day and each page, it grew a little louder.

Writing didn't magically fix everything. The darkness didn't disappear. But it gave me a way to navigate through it. It was like drawing a map of the darkest corners of my mind—marking the worst spots and the small areas where I could find some peace.

Isha, I hope you never find yourself in this darkness. But if you do, know this—you are stronger than you realize, even when it feels like you aren't.

It's okay to be scared. It's okay to take time. It's okay to fall apart.

But promise me this—don't disappear. Stay. Even if it's just for one more hour, one more sunrise, one more laugh. Stay.

Be patient with yourself. Because somewhere in that darkness, there will always be something worth holding on to. Maybe it's a memory, maybe it's a dream, maybe it's just the sound of a pen scratching against a page.

And when the time comes, when the weight feels unbearable, when you don't think you can take another step forward—just do one thing.

Reach out.

No matter what the voice in your head says, no matter how alone you feel—reach out. To me. To your mother. To someone.

Even if all you can manage is a whisper, Isha—let the world know you're still here.

Because I promise you, it's listening.

Appā

Part 4: The Things That Stay

(belonging, memory, continuity)

Isha, some things never leave us. They stay, woven into who we are, whether we hold onto them by choice or because they refuse to be forgotten. Some are comforting—like the language we grew up hearing, the stories that shaped us, the places that still feel like home even after we've left. Others are harder to carry—memories that resurface without warning, attachments to things that no longer serve us, or the echoes of people we once were.

This section is about those things—the pieces of life that linger. The things we keep, the things we return to, and the things that remind us of who we have been. As you move through your own life, you will learn that not everything that stays is meant to be held onto. Some things remain to guide us. Others, to remind us how far we have come. Only you will know which is which.

Cricket

Isha,

Cricket grabbed me early and never let go. It's not just something I watch or play—it's a part of me. And this is not just for me but for millions across the world; cricket is more than a pastime; it's a way of life, a shared language of hope and heartbreak. Your mother's father and I share this passion. I get emotional when I watch very close games, and yes, I cry watching sports. It just happens. Even years later, reruns of certain matches still grip me.

There are many games like that. One from recent times is the India-Pakistan T20 match, 2022, played in Melbourne. I sat in your grandparents' living room, hands gripping the chair. The 19th over came, and India was 32 runs behind. My chest tightened with each ball.

In the final two deliveries of that over, Kohli struck—one straight over the bowler, the other flicked off his legs. I heard the crack of the bat. Silence. Then the roar. Pure magic. I jumped, my phone slipping from my pocket but not bothering to pick it up, and then I dropped to my knees and cried. India managed to win that game that night, and I couldn't sleep. It felt like redemption, a personal victory of sorts. It was a victory for the nation. And for a week after that, the talk was just about that game, at least in my world.

Cricket didn't enter my life immediately—it crept in slowly, and then, at seven, it made its mark. I remember it vividly. 4 AM, 1985. Our TV lit the darkroom during the Benson & Hedges series in Australia. Dad was hunched over, adjusting the antenna. I was transfixed by a new world unfolding before me.

The '83 World Cup? I missed it entirely. Back then, we didn't have a TV at home, and I have no memories of that victory—strange, I know. But that '85 series got to me. Dad's eyes lit up with each play. The commentators' voices filled our quiet home, and those vast Australian stadiums became a backdrop to my growing connection with cricket—and with Dad.

Dad would watch until 6 AM before leaving for work, and I would stay glued to the TV until school time. In the evenings, he'd ask, "What happened today?" We didn't talk much, but cricket gave us words. But cricket gave us language. I'd list the scores and describe the wickets. His small nods meant everything to me. Those conversations weren't just about cricket; they were about connection.

Cricket became our language. We didn't need many words. Through the game, we understood each other. I began scribbling down the scores, eager to share updates with him.

Your grandfather loved cricket until the very end. In his last days, as he lay in bed, India was playing in Australia. A couple of days before he died, India won in Perth. He was on his deathbed, and the TV in his room had cricket on the whole night—it was a South Africa game. I stayed with him all night. That morning, my elder brother came up and told him the news. I think he liked that. Even with his eyes still closed, he smiled. Cricket became something else that day—not a game, but a familiar part of life, giving a final comfort. Every time I watch the highlights of that game now, I think of my father's last days. Bless his soul.

You may wonder why it matters to me so much. Growing up in India, it does. Cricket is everywhere. Kids play in narrow alleys with taped-up balls. Shops blare commentary. You don't need much—a stick, a wall—Cricket finds a way.
No other sport does that.

In India, cricket isn't just a game—it's a language that unites millions. Whether it's kids playing in the streets or families glued to their TVs during a World Cup, it's a shared experience that transcends age, class, and politics.

I played all the time, running around and just being outside. My skin was darkened from days spent under the sun, and my knees perpetually scraped. My mother always complained that my skin was burnt, and she was probably right. But back then, we didn't know about sunscreen or UV rays. We just played. I was an opening batsman at school—not because I was the best, but because there was a superstition about getting out early when you opened. I liked facing that first ball's uncertainty. I was very short for my age until I reached year 10, and that's when I picked up bowling. I bowled a decent medium pace, and I began liking it more than batting. Bowling gave me control; I could dictate terms. But then there were days when I was trashed around the park. That's when cricket transforms. It teaches things.

Cricket has taught me many things, Isha. Long defensive spells showed me patience. Tough losses taught me to come back. One ball changes everything. You step back in after being bowled out.

I learned more from cricket failures than wins. Failure on the field taught me resilience—the kind you carry long after the game ends—that you always show up even after a big loss.

Some losses hit hard. When my favorite team loses horribly, I avoid the news for days. I refuse to look at the scorecards as though avoiding them might soften the blow. But then the next match always pulls me back. Cricket swings between joy and frustration. It mirrors life that way. It's a good gauge of how one handles life's ups and downs. And it's very evident that I'm writing these letters after I was on the cusp of a stupid decision to end it all. Cricket opened me up about how to handle failures long ago; I just couldn't read between the lines then.

Your connection to cricket might be different from mine, just as my love for the game was different from your grandfather's. But that's how legacies evolve—each generation finds its own meaning in the things we pass down. You asked me the other day why I have cricket on all the time. I smiled but didn't answer. I don't know why, but it's just the way I am. It's a simple game—one side scores and the other tries to match it. That's all. But between the scoring and matching, life, emotions, and a nation's pride unfold.

Your aunt, my second sister, followed her cricket passion for many years. She played for the state of Karnataka before moving to Australia. And now, league cricket has taken over, with our family divided between Chennai Super Kings and Bangalore. The game has a hold on all of us.

The game isn't going anywhere, Isha. It's in your genes.

Isha, you'll face your own challenges. Maybe not cricket, but your own tough spots. Remember, it's not about winning every time. It's about the next ball, the next day.

When we watch cricket, we look beyond the scores. Each player has fought back from setbacks. Players are subject to commentary on their performance on a global scale; on a bad day, one is thrown out to the sheds, and on good days, are placed on a pedestal. I am amazed how they manage it at all and still turn up to play the game the next day. Whatever game you are into, you'll have your wins and losses, too; keep playing your game.

That's why cricket matters. It's been there through good days and bad, a constant companion. Cricket isn't just a game for me. The sound of a bat on a ball doesn't just remind me of a match—it brings back a flood of memories. The 2010 India-Australia test series, for example, is forever tied to the breakdown of my marriage and the nights I spent staying with a friend. When India lifted the World Cup in 2011, I celebrated alone, the victory bittersweet, a stark contrast to the joy around me. The iconic desert storm game in Sharjah takes me back to a pub with a close friend, both of us worried about our uncertain futures. And the final day of the 2005 Edgbaston test is linked to my time traveling in Thailand, a place of both escape and reflection. Each match marks a moment in my life. Cricket has always been there—marking moments of joy, loss, and everything in between.

You might not love cricket like I do. That's fine. Find something that grips you, teaches you to keep going, to work with others, to handle wins and losses.

Cricket still surprises me. New talents emerge. Matches turn on one ball. You never know what's coming, but you face it. It's the game's greatest lesson: be ready for the unexpected.

Dad passed cricket to me. I pass it to you. But it's not the game I hope you keep. It's the spirit of getting back up, the resilience of playing on.

Maybe for you, it won't be cricket. Maybe it will be music, or stories, or something you haven't even discovered yet. But whatever it is, Isha, I hope it teaches you what cricket taught me—how to keep going, even when the world knocks you down. I wonder, what will be your game? What will be the thing that carries you through, the thing that makes you feel alive even when life feels heavy? And when you stumble—because you will, as we all do—how will you find the strength to stand again?

Whatever you love, remember—Life is like cricket. You get a turn to bowl at what life throws at you, and you will get to bat. You never know what you will get. But when you get it, be at your best to play. It has nothing to do with luck. Luck is nothing but preparedness for coming face to face with an opportunity. Every ball counts. Every moment is special.

I don't want to make everything a lesson to take; sometimes, it just is. Love the game, any game for that matter; just be in it for the love of it. Nothing else matters after that.

Yours always, Appā

India

Isha,

You are growing up in an Australian household, surrounded by the familiar comforts of this country, but our heritage, undeniably Indian, lives within you, too. It's a thread that ties us together—one I feel deeply, even as the years of living outside India accumulate. For you, India may not carry the same gravity it does for me. You don't have the umbilical connection I do—the smells, the tastes, the sounds that shaped my childhood. India is in my body, my thoughts, my speech, and even in the sport I cheer for. For you, though, India may feel more distant instead of the loud presence it is for me.

And yet, India is no longer the home I once knew. After living more than a quarter of my life outside its borders, the land now greets me as a guest.

People in India point out how I speak differently, how my mannerisms have changed, or how I hold a knife and fork too naturally. "You're so Western now," they say, with a mix of admiration and derision. In Australia, it is the same. A simple question like, "Who do you support in cricket, Australia or India?" may sound like a simple question, but it never is. It's not just curiosity—it's a quiet test, a reminder that I don't fully belong to either side. It's a question layered with meaning, as if each answer demands a declaration of loyalty, a choice I've never been able to make. These reminders of my in-between status don't just come from questions; they also linger in the everyday details of my life, like the language I speak or the meals I cook.

It's as though both countries claim me, yet neither fully accepts me. I belong everywhere and nowhere at once.

Isha, you won't face this same judgment. You are Australian through and through. But that ease, while freeing, will come with its own losses. You won't feel the pull of Tamil phrases weaving through conversations or the warmth of biting into a soft, hot dosa at a roadside stall while motorbikes zip by. These moments are more than memories—they're threads of belonging. Without them, you might never know what it feels like to hold two places in your heart, always torn between belonging and unbelonging. This duality is my life. This has been my reality. I'm not quite Indian anymore, but never entirely Australian. I've become part of a growing group of people who don't fit cleanly anywhere—a tribe of migratory pariahs who must carve their own place between identities... It's a paradox, one of privilege and contradiction. Even as both countries question my place, my love for them remains undiminished.

Both countries call me their own. Both countries question if I truly belong. In India, I am not Indian enough. In Australia, I am not Australian enough. It is a contradiction, a dilemma, and yet also my reality. I live in the hope that acceptance might someday come naturally, though I have learned to carry the weight of being an outsider without letting it crush me.

But India, Isha, is more than a country to me. It's a paradox, chaotic and enduring. The streets of India pulse with an energy that defies comprehension—honking cars, bleating goats, the aroma of roasting peanuts mingling with the metallic tang of diesel fumes. Crowded markets burst with color: stacks of yellow turmeric, garlands of marigold flowers, and saris that shimmer like sunlight on water. To an outsider, it may seem overwhelming—a relentless tide of sights, sounds, and smells.

Yet, amid this chaos, there is a strange rhythm, a deep order that only reveals itself to those who stop trying to impose logic on it.

Somehow, everything works. The cows lying serenely in the middle of the road are never hit. The vendors who seem to argue relentlessly over a handful of rupees always resolve things in the end. It's a kind of magic that outsiders will never fully understand. They see only the surface—the noise, the disorder—but they miss the undercurrent of resilience, the way people make life work, day after day, with joy and grace. But to me, it's home—a rhythm that taught me resilience, patience, and joy in the unexpected.

In India, time doesn't flow like it does here in Australia. It stretches and folds, becoming something entirely different. A simple task, like buying a train ticket, can take hours. But in that waiting, you hear stories, meet strangers, and experience something you wouldn't have otherwise. Life isn't linear; it's layered. You learn patience because you have no choice, and in that surrender, you find moments of beauty—unexpected kindnesses, shared laughter, and connections that defy the odds.

This is the India that lives within me. It frustrates me, humbles me, and enchants me all at once. And it's why, no matter how far I am from it, I feel its pull. I see it in the Tamil songs I hum absentmindedly, in the spices that fill our pantry, and in an instinctive way, I fold my hands into a vanakkam when greeting elders. These are small, ordinary things, but they tether me to a place that shaped me, even as I've grown beyond it.

At the same time, there is grief. I speak Tamil to my family back in India, but I know you won't—not because you've turned away from it, but because life here hasn't given you the space or need to hold it close. Like your mother, you're far from the place where the language thrives, where its rhythms fill the air in everyday life. It's not your fault; Tamil isn't something you've grown up surrounded by. There's no family here to share it with, no daily need to let its words shape your voice. Still, it remains a part of you—not in the way of fluent sentences, but in the echoes of our heritage, in the stories and history that live within you, waiting if you ever wish to explore them. Language is more than words—it's a bridge to memory and identity. I think of the words I won't hear you say in Tamil, the stories that might not pass through you the way they passed through me. And yet, I hope you'll learn Tamil someday— not out of obligation, but because it carries a part of our shared story that's waiting for you. I want you to feel that connection, however distant, to where we came from.

India taught me humility, Isha– not in grand lessons, but in the rhythm of everyday life. It taught me to share space in a crowded home and noisy streets, to find patience in the longest queues, to keep hope when the odds are odds are stacked against you, and to see wealth in things money can't buy: the joy of shared meals, laughter, and the silent, steady presence of community. These lessons are universal; they're about seeing the beauty in what's already here, and I hope to pass them on to you.

But India also taught me to let go. The very chaos that makes it magical also teaches you to release control. In its unpredictability, you learn resilience. As much as I hold it close, I have learned that my roots don't need to restrict my growth. They anchor me, but they also give me the courage to venture further.

So, Isha, remember this—you don't have to choose. Belonging doesn't come from labels like 'Australian' or 'Indian.' You are more than any one identity could hold. You can weave the threads of both—or let them fray and create something entirely your own. Belonging isn't where you're from; it's about the stories you carry and the life you choose to build. Let your identity be as fluid and layered as life itself. Let it grow and change as you do.

India may never be yours the way it's mine, and that's okay. You'll find your own connections, your own anchors, your own sense of belonging. But know this: the roots I've planted will always be there for you to explore, to question, and to make your own.

Let its chaos inspire you, its beauty humble you and its resilience teach you. And when you stand at the crossroads of your own identity, remember this: you are enough. Whether you speak Tamil or not, whether you cheer for Australia or India, whether you carry the scent of spices or tea tree oil—you are enough.

India is a part of me, Isha. And through me, it's a part of you—not as a burden, but as a seed that might grow when you're ready. Whether you hold on to it tightly or let it drift softly in the background, remember this: you are enough.

But what does belonging mean to you? Maybe it won't come from a country, but from the people you love, or the traditions you carry forward. When the world asks you to choose a side, will you? Or will you make your own place, stitched from both and neither?

I wonder, Isha, how you'll weave the threads of your heritage into the life you're building. Will you find comfort in the familiar rhythms of Tamil songs, or will you create something entirely new? And when the world questions who you are, what truths will you hold onto—not for their sake, but for your own?

Appā

Milo

Isha,

Milo, our black Cavoodle, was born in November 2010. His soft, unruly curls and gentle eyes have been with us ever since. He carries a kind of love that doesn't shout or demand; it just exists, steady and unwavering, always there. Most of our passwords still include a combination of his name and birthday—a small, quiet tribute to the role he plays in our family. I bought Milo for your mother as a Valentine's gift, a gesture born of love and a bit of impulsiveness. At the time, money was tight, and when your mother heard what I'd spent, she nearly fainted. But from the moment Milo entered our home, he became hers, and she became his mother. Their bond is something special—he looks at her like she's his entire world, and she treats him as her second child.

Milo's presence is subtle yet profound. The other day, I scrolled through the photos on my phone, and in almost every picture, there he was—lying in the background, watching quietly, just being there. His gift is his quiet companionship—a presence you only notice fully when it's gone. He doesn't have to do anything extraordinary; his presence is enough.

Every evening, when I return from work, Milo waits for me at the door. There are rare evenings when he isn't there to greet me, and on those nights, the house feels incomplete, heavier somehow, as though something vital is missing. He doesn't jump or bark in excitement; he simply stands there, his tail wagging softly, asking without words, 'You're back?' Milo follows your mother everywhere. I've watched him trail behind her like a shadow, always within reach. He goes to bed around 10 every night, curling into his usual spot. But sometimes, when your mother stays up late, Milo gets up, checks on her, and sleeps next to her. It's his way of saying, 'You're not alone.' It's these small, ordinary acts that make him extraordinary. His love is constant and unspoken, but it's there, woven into the fabric of our lives.

When you were four years old, I picked you up from daycare one afternoon. You were perched on my shoulder, and out of nowhere, you asked me what would happen when Milo died. The question startled me—not just because you'd grasped the concept of death at such a young age, but because of how calmly you processed it. "We'll get a bigger dog," you said, as though Milo could be replaced. I thought about that moment for a long time, and even now, it lingers in my mind. I don't think I have the heart to bring another dog into our lives after Milo. He's special, Isha. He's not just a pet; he's a connection, a soul that feels familiar like he's been with us in some form before.

You might find it strange, but I believe Milo carries a connection from a prior life. Something in his eyes reminds me of Tiger and Sheeba, the dogs of my childhood. They weren't pets in the traditional sense but strays adopted by the hotel staff at the quarters where we lived. Tiger was a golden retriever, and Sheeba was an Alsatian. They were gentle, treating us like family and curling up under our beds at night. They weren't street dogs but had once belonged to someone, only to be abandoned and find refuge with us.

One day, a new law was passed in Bangalore to remove stray dogs from the streets, instigated by a tourism minister eager to clean up the city. Tiger and Sheeba, though they lived within the compound of the hotel staff quarters, were among the first targets. Their closeness to the five-star hotel made them easy targets for the city's campaign to clean up its streets.

I was home when the catchers came. The dogs, sensing danger, hid under our bed, but they were dragged out despite our pleas. My father, desperate to save them, tried bargaining with the catchers. "They're family," he said. "They're not strays—they belong here with us." I'll never forget their faces—angry, desperate, and scared. That memory is etched in my mind. Their fate taught me how fragile love can be and how easily it can be taken away without warning. It's perhaps why I hold Milo so tightly in my heart—because I know what it feels like to lose.

Weeks later, on my way to school, I spotted Sheeba in a park. He recognized me and wagged his tail, coming close. But before I could reach out, my mother held me back. Sheeba wasn't the same anymore. The streets had changed him—hardened him. He'd joined a pack of stray dogs, his gentle nature replaced by a fierce survival instinct. I watched him walk away, knowing he wasn't mine anymore. It felt like losing him all over again—once when they took him and again when I realized he was never coming back. It wasn't just the loss that haunted me; it was what I saw in him that day. He turned to face another dog—a stranger—and the growl that escaped his throat sent a shiver through me. His face, once so gentle, was now full of anger, his teeth bared in a snarl I didn't recognize. It scared me in a way I didn't expect. I had never been afraid of him before, but at that moment, he was no longer the Sheeba I knew.

It took me years to accept that he was gone. But that fear stayed with me, lurking quietly. It wasn't just the fear of dogs; it was the fear of how love can change—how something so familiar can become unrecognizable. I often think of Sheeba and Tiger when I look at Milo. It's as if he carries a piece of them within as if the universe doesn't take away—it finds ways to return what we've lost in another shape. Milo replaced my fear of dogs with love, but with that love comes a new fear: the fear of losing him. It's a fragile kind of love, the kind that teaches you loss before it even happens. He gave me the courage to love, knowing it could be taken away. It's the price of loving deeply—an awareness that loss is inevitable, yet still choosing to love fully.

Every evening, as I watch him wait for me at the door, I'm reminded of how much he means to us. He doesn't ask for much, just to be noticed, to be part of the rhythm of our family. His absence on the rare days he's not there is a silence that feels almost physical. And when he follows your mother around the house, tail wagging, I see in him an unconditional loyalty that most of us struggle to find in ourselves.

He's taught me so much about the quiet power of presence, about how the smallest, most ordinary moments—a walk, a nuzzle, a glance—can carry the deepest meaning.

I believe Milo has come back to us, carrying a connection from a prior life. There's something about him—something unspoken— that makes him feel like more than just a pet. There's something in his eyes, in the way he fits into our family so seamlessly, that feels familiar—like he's always been with us in some form. It's as if life, in its mysterious way, found a way to reconnect us through him. Milo isn't just part of our family; he's part of our story—a thread that ties past, present, and future together. I treat him as more than just a pet; he's a bridge to something deeper, a connection that feels timeless, a reminder that love doesn't end— it transforms. Milo's presence feels like a continuation, not a beginning, and that's why losing him will hurt so much. He's a thread in the fabric of my life, stitched together with the memories of Sheeba and Tiger and now woven into the moments we share as a family.

Reflecting on Milo brings me to a broader understanding of mortality. When you've stood at the edge of death and turned back, as I have, every moment feels borrowed. I shouldn't have been here, Isha. There were times in my life when the odds were stacked against me when I didn't think I'd make it. But I did, and now every sunrise, every laugh, every moment with you feels like a gift.

It's strange how these thoughts often wander to the rituals we leave behind, the marks we make or choose not to make in this world. Your mother wants Milo to be buried in our backyard when his time comes. When my time comes, I wish to be cremated. No one in our family has a grave—not my parents, not my grandparents, nor anyone before them. On your mother's side, there may be a few graves, but not many. In our family, we live, and when we go, we leave behind no single place of stone to grieve.

But that's the beauty of it, Isha. We don't need graves to be remembered. We carry our memories in the stories we tell, in the lives we touch, in the love we give. The stories we played a part in will continue to be shared. The rocks we sat on will carry future generations on their backs. The sun that warmed our faces will light another's dreams. In that way, we live on—not in stone or soil, but in the continuity of life itself, in the people we loved and the lives we touched.

I will live on through you. In your laughter, your dreams, and your love, I am already immortal. I carry no fear of what comes after me because I will live on in you and through you, Isha. Through your joy, your kindness, and your courage—I'll always be here.

Death humbles us with its inevitability, reminding us that every moment we build and love is finite. And yet, for all its certainty, death is never something we fully understand. It is both an end and a beginning—a transformation that takes what we know and carries it into a realm we cannot follow. What matters is not solving its mystery but learning to coexist with it. To embrace the life it shapes by its boundaries, to find meaning in the fleetingness of our days.

I've come to accept that death is not something to conquer or fear but to live alongside. It sharpens our sense of the present, reminding us that every moment is precious precisely because it is finite. It is not a thief but a quiet teacher, showing us that letting go is as vital as holding on. When Milo's time comes, I'll bury him in our backyard, just as your mother wishes. But he won't stay there, Isha. He'll be in the way the house feels less empty because of the love he left behind, in the way we'll hold each other closer because he taught us to. That's what Milo gave me: the courage to live fully, knowing every moment is borrowed.

Milo's presence feels like a continuation, not a beginning, and that's why losing him will hurt so much. He's a thread in the fabric of my life, stitched together with the memories of Sheeba and Tiger and now woven into the moments we share as a family.

That's the thing about love, Isha. It changes shape, but it never really leaves. The ones we love stay with us—in the stories we tell, the habits we pick up without realizing, the way we hold space for others.

I wonder, who will shape you the way Milo has shaped me? Who will you carry forward in the small, ordinary ways that only you will notice? And when the time comes to say goodbye—because it will, as it does for all of us—will you be able to hold love without letting fear of loss take away its weight? Will you find the courage to love fully, even when you know it won't last forever?

When my time comes, I hope I've left you with the same courage, wrapped in the stories we've shared, the lessons I've tried to pass on, and the love that binds us. I will not be gone, Isha. I will always be with you—in the laughter we shared, the quiet moments we treasured, and the love that shaped us.

Appā

ஆசையால்—தமிழில்

என் செல்ல அம்மா,

நீ என் அன்பு மகள். என் வாழ்க்கையின் எல்லாம். இந்தக் கடிதம் வெறும் வார்த்தைகள் இல்லை. இது என் இதயம் உன்னிடம் நேரடியாக பேசும் ஒரு வழி.

தமிழில் இந்தக் கடிதம் எழுதுறது எனக்கு முக்கியம். ஏன்னா, இந்த மொழில்தான் நம்ம குடும்பம் கருதி பேசினோம், நம்ம எண்ணங்கள் பிறந்தன, கனவுகள் வளர்ந்தன, வாழ்க்கை நடந்தது. இது வெறும் வார்த்தைகள் இல்லை, நம்ம உணர்வுகளோட, உயிரோட இருந்த ஒரு மொழி. நம்ம சாப்பாடு, பழக்கம், விழாக்கள், ருசிகள்—எல்லாமே தமிழோட சேர்ந்தது. நீ ஒரு நாள் இதைப் படிக்கும்போது, இது ஒரு மொழிக்கடிகாரம் இல்லை, நம்ம வாழ்நாள்களை புரிஞ்சிக்க ஒரு கதையாக இருக்கும்.

நான் உன்கிட்ட தமிழ் பேசணும்னு ரொம்ப முயற்சி பண்ணினேன். நீ தமிழை கத்துக்கணும் மட்டும் இல்ல, அதில நினைக்கணும், அதில பேசணும், அதிலே உன்னை காணணும் நினச்சேன். ஆனா, அதை முழுமையா செய்ய முடியலை, அதுக்கு எனக்கு வருத்தம் இருக்கு. அதே நேரத்துல, இன்னும் நம்பிக்கையோட இருக்கேன்—ஒரு நாள், நீ தமிழையும், நீ யாருனும் புரிஞ்சிக்குவ. நம்ம கதைகளை உணர, நம்ம வரலாற்றை தெளிவா அறிய, இந்த மொழிதான் வழி. அதுவரைக்கும், இந்தக் கடிதம் ஒரு தொடக்கம்தான், ஒரு அறிமுகம், ஒரு ஆரம்பம்.

நான் தமிழ் பற்றிப் பேசுறேன், பெருமையா! ஆனா சின்ன வயசுல அப்படி இல்லை. பெங்களூரில் வளர்ந்ததால, என்ன

தமிழனாக உணர முடியலை. நம்ம வீட்டுல பேசுற தமிழ், நான் படிக்கிறதும், கேட்கிறதும்—ஒத்திருக்கவே இல்லை. சினிமாவிலோ, பாடல்களிலோ, செய்தியிலோ வரும் தமிழ் வேற மாதிரி இருந்தது. நம்ம வார்த்தைகள், நம்ம உச்சரிப்பு, நம்ம ஒலி—எதுவும் அதோட ஒட்டாதது. ஒரு காலத்தில, நாம்மே உண்மையிலே தமிழரா? என்பதிலே ஒரு குழப்பம் இருந்தது.

அதோட, நம்ம வீட்டில் பேசுற தமிழை நான் நிஜ தமிழா எண்ண முடியலை. அது மாறுபட்ட மாதிரி தோணிச்சு. சில நேரம் அதை மறைக்க கூட நினைத்தேன். இப்போ அதை நினைக்கும்போது பெருமை இல்லை, ஆனா அந்த நேரத்துல அது நியாயமா தோணிச்சு. நம்ம வீட்டுல "ழ" ஒழுங்கா உச்சரிக்க முடியாது. நான் கேட்காத, மற்ற தமிழர்கள் பயன்படுத்தாத வார்த்தைகளை நம்ம வீட்டில் மட்டும் உபயோகிக்கிறோம். சாப்பிடறதுக்கு "துன்னு", பாட்டிக்கு "ஆயா", இன்னும் அத்தனை வார்த்தைகள். நம்ம மொழியில மதிராசி பாஷை, காஞ்சிபுரம், ஆர்காட் கலப்பு இருந்தது. ஆனா அப்போ, அப்படி ஒரு தனி தமிழ் இருக்கிறதுனே எனக்கு தெரியாம போச்சு.

அதனால நான் குழப்பத்துல இருந்தேன். நம்ம தமிழை நம்மளே ஒப்புக்கொள்ளாமல இருந்தேன், அதே நேரத்துல தள்ளி வைக்க முயற்சி பண்ணினேன். அதுக்கு இப்போ வருத்தமாக இருக்கு, ஆனா அதே நேரத்துல ஒரு நாணமும் இருக்கு. நான் மறைக்க நினைத்ததை நினைக்கும் போதெல்லாம், அது சரியா இருந்ததா என்பதுதான் கேள்வி. பிறகு புரிஞ்சிக்க ஆரம்பிச்சேன்—தமிழ் வெறும் மொழி இல்லை, அது நம்ம முன்னோர்களின் வாழ்வு, நம்ம குடும்பத்தின் பயணம், நம்ம கதைகளின் அடையாளம்.

நம்ம மொழியை விட்டுட்டு வேற மாதிரி பேசினா, நம்ம சொந்த கதைகள், நம்ம அடையாளமே மங்கிப் போயிடும் என்பதையும் புரிஞ்சிக்க ஆரம்பிச்சேன்.

நம்ம மக்கள் இந்த மொழில்தான் வாழ்ந்தாங்க, கனவு கண்டாங்க, சந்தித்ததையும் தாங்கி தொடர்ந்து இருந்தாங்க.

இது ஒன்னும் எளிது இல்லை, ஆனா மொழியோட இணைந்திருந்ததால நம்மை பிரிக்க முடியலை. அந்த மொழியுடன் நம்மக் கலந்திருக்கிறதே நம்ம உரிமை.

அதே நேரத்துல, அங்க சேர்ந்ததுபோல நடிக்க வேற மாதிரி தமிழ் பேசினாலும், அது செயற்கையானதுதான். நானே அப்படி முயற்சி பண்ணி பார்த்ததால தான் சொல்றேன்.

அது ஒரளவுக்கு நிம்மதியா தோணிக்கலாம், ஆனா மனசுக்குள்ள அது நம்ம சொந்த குரலா இல்லனு நாமே உணர்ந்து விடுவோம். அந்த உணர்வு மறந்தே போகாது.

இஷா அம்மா, நீ எங்கிருந்து வந்திருக்கோம்னு பெருமையா இரு.

நம்ம பேசுற மொழி இலக்கியத்தில வராத கூட இருக்கலாம், நம்ம சாப்பாடு நேத்து சாதத்துல உப்பு, கருவாடு ரசம் கலக்கண மாதிரி இருக்கலாம், நம்ம உடை ஒழுங்கு, அதை அணிபது, மேல்தட்டு உலகத்தோட ஒத்திருக்கலாமோ இல்லையோ—ஆனா இதுதான் நாம. இதுதான் நம்ம.

வாழ்க்கை அழகானது. உயர்வு, இறக்கம் எல்லாம் வரும்— அதை அனுபவிக்க. வேறென்ன சொல்லலாம்?

இப்போதுதான் நான் உணர ஆரம்பிச்சேன்—எல்லாமே கொடுத்துக் கொள்ளுற ஒரு சமபந்தம்.

நீ என்ன தர்றேன்னு நினைக்கிறாயோ, அதே உலகம் திருப்பி உனக்கு தரும். நீ என்னா எதிர்பார்க்கிறாயோ, நீ யாரா இருப்பேனு நினைக்கிறாயோ—அதுவே உன் வாழ்க்கையா திரும்பி வரும்.

நன்றாக இரு, நல்லதை செய். பிரபஞ்சத்துக்கு உனக்கான திட்டம் இருக்கு, அதைப்பத்தி கவலைப்படாதே—நேரம் வரும்போது அது தானாகவே தெரியும்.

நான் உன்னை ரொம்ப நேசிக்கிறேன். எப்போதும்.

நீ எப்போதும் என் அம்மா.

உன் அப்பா.

Isha, this letter in Tamil is my way of speaking to you from the heart. I struggled with my Tamil identity, feeling disconnected and even trying to distance myself from it at times. But over the years, I've realized that our language is more than just words—it carries our history, our family, and our stories. I tried to teach you Tamil, but I know I haven't done enough. Still, I hold on to the hope that one day, you will speak it, understand it, and see yourself in it. More than anything, I want you to be proud of where you come from, embrace your roots fully, and trust that life will always find its balance when you stay true to yourself.

Part 5: The Songs We Wrote

(music, play, memory)

Isha, some moments exist outside of time. They don't belong to the past, nor do they fade into the background of memory. They stay—held in melodies, in laughter, in the rhythm of words we once sang together.

These songs are ours. They may seem simple, even silly, but they carry something precious—our shared moments, the small joys that wove themselves into the fabric of our days. I want you to remember them, not just as lyrics, but as echoes of the childhood we built together. If you ever find yourself humming one of these songs years from now, I hope it brings you back to a time when the world was just us, and the music was all that mattered.

Our Three Little Songs

These are the songs of our life, Isha. They might seem simple and silly, but they are little pieces of us—songs we sang during long car rides, on rainy days, or while cooking dinner together. These are the moments I hope you'll carry with you, the ones that will make you smile even years from now.

1. This Is My Left Hand

This was the very first song we wrote together. You were about three years old, full of giggles and boundless energy. We sang it on repeat during a road trip, and by the time we got home, it had become our song.

This is my left hand,
This is my right hand,
I put them both in the air and go BOOM BOOM BOOM BOOM
This is my left leg,
This is my right leg,
I jump up in the air and go BOOM BOOM BOOM BOOM
This is my left eye,
This is my right eye,
I close them both with my hands and go BOOM BOOM BOOM BOOM
This is my tummy,
This is my pinkaan,
I eat well every day and then go BOOM BOOM BOOM BOOM

2. The Sun Comes Up

This song came to life on a rainy evening. You asked me where
the sun had gone, and we ended up singing this little tune to pass
the time. You'd clap your hands with every "BOOM" as if to
summon the sun and moon back into the sky.

The sun comes up, and the moon goes down,
The moon comes up, and the sun goes down,
When it's rainy and cloudy,
There is no sun,
There is no moon
BOOM, BOOM, BOOM, BOOM, BOOM, BOOM, BOOM.
BOOM, BOOM, BOOM.
BOOM. BOOM.

3. Going on a Treasure Hunt

Based on the famous book:

We are going on a treasure hunt, Isha and me,
We are going to have lots of fun, you just wait and see!

Oh no!
It's starting to rain!
What can we do?

We can't just hide here,
We can't just stop here,
We can't just not go,
What do we do?
Let's get wet.
Let's splash in the rain!

We are going on a treasure hunt, Isha and me,
We are going to have lots of fun, you just wait and see!

Oh no!
We are in Gruffalo land!
What can we do?

We can't let him find us,
We can't let him chase us,
We can't let him stop us,
What do we do?

Let's tiptoe...
Let's scare him out of his sleep!

We are going on a treasure hunt, Isha and me,

We are going to have lots of fun, you just wait and see!

Oh no!
Mummy is calling us!
What can we do?

We can't go home yet,
We can't have a bath yet,
We can't just not go,
What do we do?

Let's hurry…
Let's hide behind the trees!

We are going on a treasure hunt, Isha and me,
We are going to have lots of fun, you just wait and see!

Oh no!
It's getting dark!
What can we do?

We can't turn back now,
We can't lose our way,
We can't just not go,
What do we do?

Let's be brave…
Let's follow the moonlight!

We are going on a treasure hunt, Isha and me,
We are going to have lots of fun, you just wait and see!

Oh yes!

We found the treasure!
What else can we do?

We can laugh and cheer,
We can jump and shout,
We can sing, "Hooray!"

Let's go on another hunt,
Let's find something new.

Part 6: What I Know (For Now)

(wisdom, choice, evolution)

Isha, I don't have all the answers. No one does. What I know today may shift tomorrow, and that's how it should be. Growth means questioning, re-evaluating, and allowing yourself to change. These are the truths I have come to understand, but they are not meant to bind you. They are not rules carved in stone.

Take what speaks to you. Leave what doesn't. And if, one day, you find that something I wrote no longer fits the person you've become, let it go without hesitation. My love for you does not come with conditions, and neither should the wisdom I leave behind. More than anything, I want you to live fully, to think for yourself, and to build a life that is truly yours.

Yours, Forever

You've made it this far, and I hope these letters have given you a sense of who I am—flaws, stories, love, and all. More importantly, I hope they've shown you how deeply you are loved, how fiercely I believe in you, and how proud I am of the person you are becoming.

But these letters are not meant to shape you or bind you. They are not a map of your life. You will carve your own path, make your own mistakes, and find your own truths. These words are here for one purpose: to remind you that you are not alone. In moments when you feel lost, you have a compass within you—a strength that runs through our family, through your spirit, and through these letters.

If my words ever feel heavy, let them go. If they ever prevent you from fully living your own life, burn them. I am writing to help you grow, not to confine you.

You are my miracle, my anchor, and my greatest joy. You have already taught me more about love than I ever thought I could know. Whatever life holds for you, I will always be with you—in these words, in the love I poured into raising you, and in the quiet moments we shared.

Go out into the world, Isha. Live boldly, love deeply, and keep growing into the incredible person I already know you are. The rest of your story is yours to write.

But before you go, there are a few lessons I want to leave with you—truths I've gathered from my own journey, offered to guide you when you need them most.

1. Be Grateful and Embrace Abundance

Gratitude changes everything, Isha. When you are grateful for what you have, fear and envy lose their grip. Gratitude reminds you of what truly matters and fills your life with a sense of abundance, even when life feels sparse.

Every morning, I wake up grateful for one thing: that I am alive. This practice didn't come easily. It grew out of times when everything felt impossibly hard—when loss and uncertainty left me grasping for anything to hold onto. Gratitude doesn't need something big to anchor it. Sometimes, it's as simple as noticing the softness of the pillow beneath your head or the beauty of a sunrise. It doesn't erase the pain, but it makes the weight easier to carry.

Gratitude is about seeing abundance in what you already have. We often think abundance for more—more wealth, more success, more recognition. But abundance begins in the way you see the world. It's not about how much you have but how much you appreciate.

Think of a seed. Within it, a whole tree waits to grow. A mango tree, perhaps—offering shade, fruit, and countless new seeds to plant. That's how life works—it is boundlessly abundant. But abundance only flourishes when you nurture it, and gratitude is the water that helps it grow.

Comparison is the thief of gratitude, my love. When you measure your life against others, you lose sight of the gifts in your own story. You don't need what others have to feel grateful. Gratitude begins with appreciating what is already yours, no matter how small or ordinary it may seem.

Life will offer you both scarcity and abundance, but the lens through which you see it will make all the difference. When you focus on what you lack, life feels smaller and harsher. When you focus on what you have, it expands. Gratitude transforms scarcity into abundance—not by changing what you have but by changing how you see it.

Just remember, gratitude is not passive. When life gives to you, give back. Share your abundance—whether it's your time, your love, or your resources. What you give will come back to you many times over.

So, wake up each day with a heart full of gratitude. Notice the little things that make life beautiful. Embrace the abundance that's already within and around you. And in doing so, you'll discover that life is not about what you have but how much you cherish it.

2. Give

Life is about sharing, helping, and lifting others up, Isha. Generosity brings meaning to our days and connects us to something bigger than ourselves.

I'll be honest with you—I've given too much at times. I've given to those who didn't deserve it, to situations that didn't require it, even to those who took me for granted. And yes, sometimes it drained me. But here's the thing: I never regretted it. Giving, for me, has always been a way to live in alignment with my heart. Even when it cost me dearly, I found a strange sense of fulfillment in it.

When you give, give with clarity and kindness. Don't give to seek approval or out of obligation—give because you want to. And if you ever find yourself giving reluctantly, be honest with yourself and the receiver. There's no shame in saying, "I'm doing this, but it's hard for me." Generosity shouldn't come from a place of resentment—it should come from a place of truth.

Giving isn't about the size of the gesture; it's about the spirit behind it. A kind word, a listening ear, or a moment of your time can mean more than any grand act. Sometimes, the smallest acts of generosity create the biggest ripple effects.

But I also want to caution you, my love: be mindful of your limits. Giving without boundaries can leave you empty. Your well must remain full enough to sustain yourself because you cannot give to others if you've nothing left to give to yourself.

And remember this: generosity isn't a transaction—it's a way of being. Don't give up expecting something in return, but know that life has a way of reflecting your energy back to you. When you give with love and sincerity, life responds in kind.

Give, Isha, not because it's easy or expected, but because it's who you are. Give with joy, with clarity, and with intention. And know that in your giving, you will receive something far greater than you ever imagined—not in material possessions, but in connection, meaning, and a deeper sense of yourself.

3. Celebrate Belonging

Belonging, Isha, isn't about changing yourself to fit in—it's about honoring who you are and finding the people and places that embrace you. True belonging begins within. When you accept yourself—your strengths, flaws, and all—you create the space for real connection.

Belonging isn't passive. It's built in the laughter you share with friends, the traditions you create with family, and the moments that remind you of your place in the world.

Life will pull you in many directions, Isha, but don't forget what grounds you: the people who lift you up and the places that feel like home. Celebrate those connections, nurture them, and carry that sense of belonging with you wherever you go.

4. Travel

Travel, Isha. See the world. There's nothing like stepping into the unknown to understand yourself and others.

Travel reshapes how you see life. It opens your heart to new perspectives and shows you the beauty of differences. You'll learn that the world is vast, full of stories waiting to be heard, and no matter how far you go, you'll always carry yourself with you.

Our family has come a long way, and the next generation, to which you belong, is already chasing bigger dreams that stretch further. You are part of this unfolding story.

The unknown isn't something to fear, Isha—it's where life hides its greatest gifts. Travel isn't just about places; it's about stepping into the unfamiliar, letting it change you, and coming back with a heart full of stories and a mind wide open.

So, Isha, pack your bags. Wander without a map sometimes. Let the world challenge you, inspire you, and make you whole. Life chooses you for a conspiracy when you step into the unknown, and I promise it will always be worth it.

5. Fall in Love, Cry from a Heartbreak

Fall deeply, Isha. Let love sweep you up, fully and unapologetically. Love is one of life's greatest gifts—it will show you the heights of joy and the depths of your soul.

But love isn't always forever. Sometimes, it ends. And when it does, let yourself feel it all—the pain, the grief, the heartbreak. Don't shy away from it. Heartbreak has a way of carving space within you, making room for greater compassion and understanding. It's not the end; it's a beginning—reshaping you into someone stronger, wiser, and more open to love again.

One thing I want you to remember: never marry to validate someone else's love for you. Marriage, or any commitment, should come from mutual growth and respect, not as proof of devotion. Your worth is not tied to someone else's promises—it's yours to own.

Love boldly, and don't fear its loss. If it breaks you, let the cracks teach you. Love will always be worth the risk because it teaches you how deeply you're capable of feeling.

6. Purpose will find you

Don't chase purpose, Isha—it will find you when you're ready.

There was a time in my life when I felt lost, unsure of what I was meant to do or be. After losing almost everything—my marriage, my fortune, my sense of self—I found myself standing on the edge of life's darkest moments. I wasn't searching for purpose then; I didn't have the strength. Instead, I began to write—not to sound like Rushdie or Bukowski, but simply to hear my own voice.

With each word, I found clarity. And in that clarity, purpose quietly revealed itself. Writing became my anchor, not because I went looking for it, but because I allowed myself to live fully in the present moment.

Purpose isn't a destination. It's not something you pursue or force. It unfolds naturally when you are true to yourself—when you stop comparing, stop chasing, and start trusting the path life is carving for you.

Live with curiosity, courage, and presence, and purpose will find you. It may arrive quietly in the things you do without realizing their significance. Trust that life will guide you, and when clarity comes, let it give you the strength to be yourself.

7. Dream

Everything that has ever been created began with a dream, Isha. Dreams are the seeds of action, the blueprints of possibility. If you can't dream it, you can't manifest it.

When you allow yourself to dream boldly, you open doors to worlds beyond what you know. Dreams give life its direction—they're the whispers of what could be, waiting for you to bring them to life.

But dreaming is only the first step. A dream without action remains a wish. Nurture your dreams with effort, persistence, and faith. You don't need to chase perfection; what matters is daring to take the first step.

The beauty of dreaming is that it's uniquely yours. What you imagine, what you strive for, will reflect your spirit and desires. So dream freely, dream fully, and remember: every great thing begins in the quiet space where vision meets courage.

8. Life happens

Life will break you, Isha. It's not a question of if but when. The world doesn't stop for anyone's pain, and life doesn't follow a script. It will throw hardships, betrayals, and losses your way. But here's the truth: life isn't doing this to punish or reward you—it's simply life.

When life happens, you need to be strong enough to let it flow through you without losing yourself. Strength doesn't mean you won't feel pain. It doesn't mean you won't stumble or question everything. Strength is about letting those experiences shape you without breaking your spirit.

We're here to experience life—not control it. Through us, life experiences itself: the joys, the challenges, the unexpected. That's our purpose—not to resist life but to embrace it fully.

When life bends you, let it. When it breaks you, rebuild yourself. Don't fight the cracks—let them show you where growth is happening. The cracks aren't failures; they're the markers of a life fully lived.

You are not here to conquer life. You're here to feel it, endure it, and grow through it. When the world feels overwhelming, remember life happens to everyone, but the way you respond is where your power lies.

9. Every choice you make has consequences

Every choice you make, Isha, shapes your life in ways you may not always foresee. Some consequences will be immediate, while others will unfold slowly, quietly altering your path. What matters most is not avoiding these outcomes but owning them.

If you make a mistake, admit it. If your choice hurts someone, apologize. And if your decision leads to something beautiful, embrace it with gratitude. Trying to hide from the consequences of your actions only delays the lessons they carry and keeps you from growing.

Life isn't about getting everything right. It's about learning, adapting, and continuing to move forward. Be bold in your choices and honest in facing their results. Accept, admit, and embrace what comes.

The life you create, Isha, will be the sum of your choices and their consequences. Own them all—they will make you who you are.

10. Forgiveness is a Choice

Forgiveness, Isha, is one of the hardest choices you'll ever make, but it's also one of the most freeing. Forgiveness isn't about letting someone else off the hook—it's about releasing the hold their actions have on you.

It's not easy. I know this because I've tried—and I'm still trying. There were times I thought I'd forgiven, only to feel anger rise again when a word, a memory, or an image dragged me back to the moment of betrayal. Even after losing my marriage, my fortune, and my sense of self—I'd think I'd moved on, only to realize how deeply the hurt still lived within me.

Anger doesn't stay contained. It seeps into unexpected corners of your life, shaping decisions, creating distance, and clouding your peace.

Forgiveness doesn't erase those feelings overnight—it demands revisiting them, facing them, and choosing to let go over and over again. Anger doesn't stay contained. It seeps into unexpected corners of your life, shaping decisions, creating distance, and clouding your peace.

Forgiveness is for you. It doesn't mean forgetting or excusing a betrayal. Remember the lesson, let it sharpen your instincts, and set boundaries where they're needed. But don't let the hurt define you.

Take your time with forgiveness, Isha. It's not a moment but a journey. Choose it for your own sake, at your own pace. When you're ready, forgiveness will bring you peace.

11. Read

Books, Isha, hold the wisdom of lifetimes. When you open one, you're not just reading words—you're stepping into someone else's world, walking paths they've tread, and learning lessons they've preserved for you.

I didn't grow up in a home filled with books. My parents didn't have proper schooling, and reading wasn't a part of our lives. I wasn't just starting at base zero; I was starting from minus four. Because of that, I started far behind others, not even knowing the importance of books until college. But when I discovered reading, it was like the world opened up to me in ways I never imagined.

What's magical about books is that they meet you where you are. Two people can read the same book and walk away with completely different lessons because books adapt to the reader's perspective. That's their power—they aren't fixed; they're alive.

So read widely, my love. Let books open your mind, challenge your thinking, and transform your spirit. They are doorways to worlds, ideas, and truths waiting for you to discover.

12. Ditch Perfection

Don't aim to be perfect, Isha—aim to be real.

The world will try to convince you that being whole means always being compassionate, agreeable, or joyful. But perfection is a trap that keeps you stuck, anxious, and afraid of failure. Life doesn't exist in those extremes. It thrives in the messy, in-between spaces where mistakes are made, lessons are learned, and growth happens.

I've tried to live authentically, and it hasn't always been easy. The world will push you to pick a side, to conform to ideals that feel too small for the fullness of who you are. Don't let it. Embrace the friction because it's in that tension that you'll find your unique balance.

Remember, the cracks in your foundation don't weaken you—they make you human. And being real, not perfect, is what makes life worth living.

13. Never deny your identity

Stand proudly for who you are.

The other day, I was at the grocery store, waiting for my turn at the cash counter. The man ahead of me tried to make small talk with the cashier, but it wasn't going anywhere. Then the man asked, "Are you Nepalese?" The cashier replied firmly, "No. My name is Alan."

That seemed to end the conversation. Silence followed, awkward and heavy. The man gave me a polite smile, then turned away, making no further effort to connect. But halfway through weighing a bag of mandarins, the cashier looked up and said, "Yes, I'm from Nepal."

The silence broke. The air shifted.

The man's face lit up as if he'd won a small victory. He turned to me with a triumphant smile, then eagerly resumed talking to the cashier. The cashier, who'd been avoiding eye contact, finally looked up, smiled, and exchanged a few words in another language—probably Nepalese.

What happened in those moments? Between denying his identity and affirming it, something shifted. It wasn't just a conversation— it was a quiet battle. A question of identity, courage, and the strength it takes to acknowledge who we are.

I have noticed at school, you refuse to call me Appā, and you admonish me for calling you my Amma—you think it's not cool. One day, when you had to present something about your culture, you chose not to show them the video of you celebrating Ganesha's birthday—despite all the effort you put into the arrangements. Instead, you spoke about your Easter holiday.

Despite your mother's insistence that you speak and show your classmates the video of you enjoying yourself at Ganesha's birthday celebration, you refused. You remarked that your friends would laugh at you.

But these small things add up. Each time you hold back a part of yourself, you will lose grounding in who you are. Trust me. I gave up on my Tamil heritage and stayed away from it for so long—now I'm doing a lot of catching up to learn it.

No matter where you go, you will always be a girl of South Indian heritage. Accept it. When you do, it frees your mind for other, far more important things.

Denying only takes you so far. But at some point, you look around and realize that all the denial in the world didn't bring you closer to belonging—it only took you further from yourself

Isha, your identity is not just a name or a nationality—it's the culmination of generations who came before you. Even if there are parts of your heritage that feel complicated or imperfect, don't deny them. To deny your identity is to deny the story of those who carried you to this moment.

But identity is not just inherited—it's created. While you honor where you come from, also take the responsibility to shape who you want to be. Build an identity that reflects your truth, one that the next generation can proudly carry forward.

You are not just the product of your past—you are the author of your future.

14. Choose your labels carefully

L Labels define, but they can also confine. Be careful with the words "I am," Isha. What follows them shapes not only how the world sees you but how you see yourself.

You'll find many labels in life: some you're born with, like being Tamil, Australian, Woman, or a Person of Color. Others will come from family, friends, or society. But labels are boundaries—they come with expectations and assumptions. Don't rush to accept them. Take your time to understand who you are and reject anything that doesn't feel true to you.

The freedom to define yourself is a gift. Use it wisely, my love.

15. Go dance. Seek bliss

Imagine a world without humans, Isha. The rivers would still carve their paths, flowers would still bloom, and the trees would sway in the breeze. Nature's rhythm is effortless, and there's a lesson in that: life is about being, not striving.

We spend so much time worrying about the past or imagining the future that we forget to live. But the present moment is where life actually happens. Feel the sun on your skin, taste the sweetness of fruit, and let yourself simply be. That's where contentment lies— not in chasing perfection but in embracing life's beautiful complexity.

Bliss isn't the same as happiness. Happiness often depends on something external—a person, a moment, or an achievement. But bliss comes from within. It's in the act of dancing, writing, painting, or creating—things that make you feel alive, whether or not anyone is watching.

So go dance, my love. Write, paint, sing, and play. Let your joy bloom like a flower, free and untamed. In that bliss, you'll find the truest version of yourself.

16. If you said it, own it

Words carry weight, Isha. Once spoken, they leave an imprint—on others and on yourself. If your words were wrong, admit it. Apologize sincerely. It takes strength to say, "I was wrong," and even more to learn from it.

If your words were right, stand by them. Defend your truth with confidence but without malice. Never lie about what you didn't say—it only creates distrust and pain.

What you say reflects who you are. Choose your words carefully, but once spoken, own them fully.

17. What you are is what you get

Life mirrors you, Isha. The energy you put out into the world—kindness, love, curiosity, or fear—comes back to you. If you want trust, be trustworthy. If you want love, be loving.

I've seen this in my own life. When I was guarded and unsure, the people around me reflected that same energy. But when I chose openness and kindness, the world opened to me.

Be the person you want to welcome into your life. What you are is what you get. You get what you give.

18. Burn your beliefs

Let go of what no longer serves you. Question everything. Life is a journey of discovery, and to truly discover, you must be willing to rethink, evolve, and even let go of long-held beliefs.

Belief can feel comforting, but it stifles self-inquiry. It stops you from questioning and knowing. Instead, doubt. Explore. Keep asking questions until you find your own truth.

When you reach a place of knowing—something discovered, not handed to you—you will stand rooted, unshaken. Beliefs can bind you, but knowing sets you free.

19. Don't try to be a Buddha

Life isn't about becoming perfect or enlightened. It's about being fully present in this moment.

Sometimes, we get caught up in trying to reach some higher state, thinking it will bring clarity or peace. But the truth is, peace comes when you stop striving and simply allow life to flow.

Sit quietly sometimes. Don't judge, don't label—just observe. In those moments of stillness, you'll glimpse the space where everything simply exists as it is. That's enough.

You don't have to be a Buddha, my love. You just have to be you.

20. Burn this book if it gets in your way

Burn these letters if they ever stop you from living fully. These words are not sacred—they are just my reflections, meant to guide you, not bind you.

No single book, no single idea, not even these lessons, can capture the fullness of life. If my words ever feel like a cage, set them free. Burn them.

Your life is yours to discover. Read, learn, and grow—but never let anything, including this book, keep you from living your truth.

21. Don't follow me

These letters are here to show you my journey, not to map out yours.

Your life will be uniquely yours, filled with questions I never asked and answers I never found. Let my reflections be a starting point, not a doctrine. Burn them if they ever feel like a weight.

You are not here to walk in my footsteps. You are here to carve your own path. Trust yourself. That's your journey. Let my journey be a starting point, but never let it confine you.

Closing Reflection:

Isha, these lessons are the essence of my journey—offered to you with all the love and sincerity I can muster. They are not rules or demands but reflections of what I've learned, shaped by the moments that made me and the mistakes that humbled me.

You are not here to follow my path but to carve your own. These words are meant to guide you when you need them, to remind you of the strength you carry, and to offer comfort in the moments you feel lost. But if they ever feel like a weight, let them go. These lessons are not what makes your life meaningful and beautiful— you already hold everything you need within yourself.

Your story, my love, is yours to write. The rest of your life stretches ahead of you, waiting to be explored, felt, and lived with all the boldness, grace, and curiosity I already know you possess.

Live boldly, love deeply, and be true to yourself. The world will test you, and it won't always be kind. But it will also surprise you, inspire you, and make you laugh when you least expect it. Hold on to those moments, Isha. They will remind you why it's all worth it.

I will always be with you, not just in these letters but in every memory we've created and every quiet moment we've shared. You are my greatest joy, my deepest love, and my proudest legacy.

Go live, Isha. This is your time.

Love forever,
Appā

Isha,

When I began these letters, I thought I was offering you a guide. But I see now—I was offering myself one, too.

Some days, the words came easily. Other days, I erased them, wondering if they were worth leaving behind. But if I've learned anything, it is this: love isn't about having all the answers. It is about showing up. In uncertainty. In silence. In the spaces where words fail.

You will live your own story. You will love, lose, break, and rebuild. And I will not always be there to guide you. But these words will.

If ever you find yourself searching, Isha—know this: you were always loved. And love is enough. It will be enough.

"தந்தை மகற்காற்று நன்றி அவையத்து முந்தி இருப்பச் செயல்."

"The duty of a father is to prepare his child to stand strong among the wise."

— Kural 67, Thirukkural, Tiruvalluvar (circa 5th century CE)

Your Appā will always be with you, in these words, in your laughter, in the quiet spaces where love lingers long after I am gone.

About the Author

Veera Raghavan is a storyteller who balances life as a financial professional by day and a writer by night. His work explores the messy, beautiful truths of love, loss, fatherhood, and belonging. Born into one world and making a home in another, Veera's journey has been shaped by migration, identity, and the weight of memory. His words—whether in poetry or prose—capture the contradictions of life: the ache of absence, the beauty of resilience, and the quiet ways love endures.

When he's not working with numbers, Veera finds meaning in life's smallest, most fleeting moments—cooking dinner, packing school lunches, or watching his daughter play with her imaginary friends, fully aware of her father sitting nearby, smiling as he shares in the magic of the world she is creating.

This book, a collection of letters to his daughter, is more than a testament to love—it is a record of survival, a reckoning with the past, and a father's attempt to leave behind something real.

www.ingramcontent.com/pod-product-compliance
Lightning Source LLC
Chambersburg PA
CBHW060358310726
48976CB00003B/864